Tracey Jane Jackson

Bound By Joy

A Cauld Ane Christmas Novella

Bound by Joy is a work of fiction. Names, characters, places, and incidents are the products of the author's imagination and are used fictitiously. Any resemblance to actual events, locales, or persons, living or dead, is entirely coincidental.

Cover Photo
Couple:
Tracey Jane Jackson

Landscape:
Stock Photo

Cover Art
Jackson Jackson

Cover Models
Scott Stevens
Shana Kunze

ISBN: 978-1517257521

Published in the United States

I've followed Tracey Jane Jackson's Cauld Ane series from book one and am constantly impressed by the way her characters keep growing and developing. Her dialogue is realistic and witty and her fast-paced storylines keep the series progressing nicely. I've enjoyed each Bound book, but Bound by Dreams is my favorite so far. I can't wait to see what happens next! _Amanda Washington:_ _Author of the Perseverance Series and the Chronicles of the Broken Series_

This series is one I will be getting paperbacks to keep on my LOVE bookshelf and one I will be rereading many, many times!! This deserves more than just 5+++ stars, but since it is the highest rating it will let me give, it will have to do. _Amazeballs Book Addicts_

Booklist

Cauld Ane Series

Bound by Blood
Cauld Ane #1

Bound by Fire
Cauld Ane #2

Bound by Secrets
Cauld Ane #3

Bound by Song
Cauld Ane #4

Bound by Dreams
Cauld Ane #5

Bound by Tears
Cauld Ane #6

Bound by Light
Cauld Ane #7

Bound by Joy
A Cauld Ane Christmas Novella

Civil War Brides Series

The Bride Price
Civil War Brides Series, Book #1

The Bride Found
Civil War Brides Series, Book #2

The Bride Spy
Civil War Brides Series, Book #3

The Bride Ransom
Civil War Brides Series, Book #4

The Rebel Bride
Civil War Brides Series, Book #5

The Bride Star
Civil War Brides Series, Book #6

The Bride Pursued
Civil War Brides Series, Book #7

The Bride Accused
Civil War Brides Series, Book #8

The Brides United
Civil War Brides Series, Book #9

Acknowledgements

Ása Erlingsdóttir, thanks again for the Icelandic translations!

Scott & Shana - you guys are beautiful inside and out!

Thanks to Ellen, Amanda, and Roslyn for the edits and critiques...
you guys are amazing!

Dedication

May your Christmas be filled with love and blessings!
Thanks for being such amazing readers!

CHAPTER ONE

Two Years Ago...

Edinburgh, Scotland

KENNA MCFADDEN WALKED into her sister's home... her home, for the time being anyway...and fell into Gillian's hug. She was on hiatus from her job as tour manager for the multi-platinum album selling band, Fallen Crown, and she desperately needed the break. "Och, sis, I'm knackered."

Gillian gave her a squeeze. "You're always knackered when you're done with a tour."

Kenna sighed with relief, looking forward to reconnecting with her family...finally. "Aye, 'tis true. I can't wait for the next year off."

"Max is givin' you a year, is he?"

"That's what he said." She smiled. "I still have my job with Rogue, but it'll only be a couple of days a week for now." Rogue was a non-profit company the leaders of Fallen Crown, Niall and Max, started to aid and protect human women and children in abusive situations. Kenna helped women settle into their new lives, using her gift of suggestion to calm often volatile situations. "You know what Rogue is like, it's feast or famine, so the hours are unpredictable. Plus, besides her normal duties, Grace is taking over a lot of the tour management, so it's all good."

Max's mate, Grace, was now working for Kenna as her assistant and Kenna loved her. She also loved knowing that if she ever wanted to leave her job permanently, she'd be leaving the band in Grace's capable hands.

"Are you all right with your job essentially being eliminated?"

"Aye, love. Very much so. It's a good time to transition out, anyway. I can concentrate on Rogue and perhaps spend more time with you."

"Well, I for one am so glad you're home," Gillian said.

"Me too, love. With all the drama with Max, I'm especially drained."

Gillian sighed. "I can't believe he thought something to do with Moira's death."

Max and Niall's sister, Moira, had been Kenna's closest friend until Moira was brutally murdered. Max had somehow gotten in his mind that Kenna had lured her to her death and had spent more than a hundred years hating her for it. They'd just recently sorted through their issues and things were now forgiven.

"Max has always been a bit of a prick."

Kenna giggled. "Thank God for Grace."

"Aye...a thousand times, yes. Thank God for Grace."

Kenna bit back a yawn. "I finally have enough time to find a home of my own."

"You're not goin' anywhere until yer bound...or I'm bound," Gillian countered. "Last standing spinster gets the house."

Kenna giggled. "How old are we now?"

"I stopped counting at two hundred."

"Exactly." Kenna waved her hand in the air. "I doubt we're going to find our mates any time soon."

"One can dream, dear heart."

"Aye. One can certainly dream."

Gillian grabbed a suitcase and started toward the stairs. "Let's get you settled. I made stew if you're hungry."

"You made me stew?"

"Aye, why?"

"You're just the best sister ever."

Gillian laughed. "Oh, if only you'd said that when we were wee."

"I'm sure I did. A thousand times."

"Never. Not once," Gillian corrected.

"Well, I'm saying it now."

Gillian grinned as she pushed open the guest room door. Kenna stepped inside, throwing the bag she carried onto the bed while Gillian set the other one near the door.

"Do you want to eat or sleep?"

Kenna nodded.

Gillian chuckled. "Come and eat then, and when you've had enough I'll leave you to sleep."

"Thank you."

Kenna followed her sister downstairs and helped herself to dinner. "Any news from Payton?"

Their sister was mated to Brodie Gunnach, one of the princes of the Cauld Ane, and she was expecting their first child. She was due any day now and Gillian and Kenna had promised to be there for the birth.

"No. She's just feeling huge and wanting the baby out."

Kenna sighed. "She is big, eh?"

"Aye, but look at Brodie, you can't exactly call him small."

"Will she be okay?"

"Aye, love, she'll be fine. Our babies are usually big."

Kenna sat at the table and frowned. "How's Brodie going to take all of this?"

Gillian laughed. "He's going to completely lose his mind, but that's part of the reason we're going to be there."

"Aye, I suppose 'tis."

Gillian poured herself a glass of wine and handed Kenna a Belhaven. "Eat yer supper and don't worry about Pay. We'll take good care of her."

Kenna grinned with a nod, sipping the beer. "Thank you."

* * *

Kenna awoke as the buzz of her cell phone busted into her dream. Ewan MacGregor was leaning in to kiss her after admitting his undying love for her. Of course, he wasn't married with kids in her dream, because it was long before his wife had even been born.

"Hello," she grumbled.

"Oh, Kenna," a worried Alaina Meyer rasped. "Can you come in, please? We need your help."

Kenna glanced at the clock. Three a.m. "What's going on, love?"

"A human woman came in with her two kids and we're having difficulty handling the husband."

Kenna sat up and threw the covers off. "The husband's *there*?"

"Aye."

"And everyone's in Inverness," Kenna finished.

Max and Grace's main home was in the Scotland countryside, and Niall and Charlotte were visiting for a few weeks. Alaina's voice hitched. "Aye."

"What about Dalton or Cole?"

"I've left messages for both of them."

"Okay, love, I'll be there in fifteen minutes." Kenna hung up and rushed to dress. She left a note for her sister, grabbed her keys, and headed out to the car. She wasn't far from Rogue House, and at this hour, there was no traffic. Thank God for small favors.

Arriving at the back entrance of the Rogue offices, Kenna locked her car and rushed inside. She could hear the slurred bellow of a deep voice coming from the conference room near the lobby, so she made her way there. She walked inside to find a disheveled and filthy man, hands cuffed behind his back, sitting on the floor with his cuffs secured to a bolt in the concrete.

Dalton Moore leaned against the wall with his arms crossed, his gun visible but still holstered. Dalton was the king's brother-in-law, but he was also human and worked closely with the human side of the Cauld Ane security company. He was ex-FBI, American, and although he was model gorgeous, he was equally as scary when he had to be. He caught sight of Kenna and gave her a chin lift. "Hey."

"Hi," Kenna said. "Are the police on their way?"

"Yes."

"Who the hell are you?" the man yelled.

"Shut your mouth," Dalton demanded.

"Are you the bitch who kidnapped my family?"

Kenna frowned.

Dalton stepped in front of him, blocking his view of Kenna. "You speak to me not her."

"I *will* find them," the man seethed, and leaned to the right in order to see Kenna. "Then I'll find you."

Even though the man was human and would never be able to match Kenna's strength, she couldn't stop a shiver.

Dalton shifted again then faced her. "Safe room."

Kenna nodded. "Thanks."

She left as fast as she could and headed through the complicated maze of hallways and false walls and doors that led to one of three safe rooms. Each entrance could only be accessed through thumbprint and swipe card security panels, so even if someone found their way to one of the doors, they wouldn't be able to get inside.

Kenna and three other people who'd worked for Rogue for more than twenty years were the only ones with access, plus Niall, Max, and their mates, which provided an extra level of security.

Sixth door in, she turned left and walked into the safe room open on the schedule. Alaina sat on one of the sofas holding a very thin toddler while a young woman, beaten and bloody, huddled in the opposite corner, a dirty young boy in her lap.

"Hi," Alaina whispered.

"Hi. Has everyone been fed?"

"Cook's making something for them now."

"Thank you." Kenna smiled gently and sat on the coffee table across from the woman. "How are you, lass?"

"Who are you?" the little boy demanded, obviously trying to protect his mother.

"My name's Kenna, sweetheart. Can you tell me your name?" She reached her hand out to shake his hand. If he'd touch her, she could get him to do whatever she needed him to with her gift of suggestion.

"It's Donnall. I'm named after me father," he said proud-ly, and took her hand.

"Well, that's a very fine name."

"I want me da."

"I know, love, but I'm afraid he's not up to visitors right now." She laid her free hand over his and studied him. "Can I have a look at yer mummy, please? I'd like to help her feel better."

Donnall climbed from his mother's lap and sat beside Alaina who was holding his sister.

"Thank you," Kenna said, and focused on the mother. "You look pretty sore, love. Do you mind if we have you examined?"

"No," she mumbled, and then whimpered.

"She may have a broken jaw," Alaina provided.

Kenna nodded and dialed Gillian's phone.

"Kenna, you all right?" her sister asked.

"Aye. We have a woman and her two children here and I'm wondering if you can swing by and have a look at them."

"Aye, love, but not for about thirty minutes. I've just finished up with a mum and have to turn her over to Dr. Madsen, then I'll be able to leave."

"That's fine. She may have a broken jaw, is there anything I can do for her?"

"Just keep her still, love."

"I can do that."

"I'll be there as soon as I can," Gillian promised.

"Thanks."

Kenna hung up and smiled at Donnall's mother. "I'm going to grab some paper and a pen so you don't have to speak, okay?" The woman nodded and Kenna stepped into the supply closet at the back of the room. Grabbing pen and paper, she also took some crayons and coloring books from their stash and headed back to the little family. While Alaina got the kids settled with the crayons, Kenna sat in front of the woman, handing her the paper. "Can you write down your name, please?"

She nodded and scribbled, *Claire Mann.*

"It's lovely to meet you, Claire. My sister is a doctor and she's going to be here shortly to have a look at all of you and then we'll go about finding you a safe place to stay for a while. We have a flat here, and although it's safe, I don't like that your husband knows where you are."

Claire nodded, blinking back tears.

"Right, love. I'm going to check on breakfast and then find some clothes for your bairns. We'll let them have baths and get them fed and into something clean if that sounds good to you."

Claire nodded again, and wrote, *thank you.*

Kenna smiled and took the back door out of the safe room and toward the kitchen. The rest of the morning was filled with police reports, paperwork, acquiring money for Claire and her family, along with procuring a safe place where Donnall Senior couldn't find them.

By the time Kenna arrived home at almost six that night, she fell into bed and slept until ten the next morning.

* * *

Three days later, Kenna was in her bathroom, pulling her hair back in order to wash her face when Gillian appeared in the doorway. "Payton's in labor."

"Now?" Kenna asked, splashing water on her face.

"Aye. We have to get to Connall's as soon as possible."

"Why's she at Con's place?" Kenna patted her skin dry with a towel.

"There's something going on, but Niall wouldn't tell me over the phone."

"Niall's with her? Why? Where's Brodie?"

Gillian rolled her eyes. "I don't *know*, love, but we've got to go."

"Okay, keep yer knickers on," Kenna retorted. "Just have to grab my purse."

Kenna rushed to her bedroom and then down the stairs and joined her sister who was standing at the front door, waving her on.

"I haven't been a doctor for more than three hundred years for Payton to have this bloody baby without us," Gillian decreed.

Kenna giggled. "Amen, sis."

Gillian threw her medical bag in the back of her sedan and Kenna jumped into the front seat, securing her seat belt while Gillian climbed into the driver's seat.

Connall's flat wasn't far from Gillian's and she pulled into the driveway and turned off the car less than ten minutes later. Kenna was momentarily overwhelmed with feelings of love, but she shook it off, assuming the emotion was for her sister.

"Ready?" Gillian asked, grabbing her bag from the back.

"Aye. Let's meet our new bairn."

CHAPTER TWO

GUNNAR BALDURSSON SLID his phone into his pocket. He was with his brother Kaspar and Kaspar's mate, Jesska, at the home of Connall and Pepper Gunnach. They'd been dealing with conflicts between the Scottish Cauld Ane and Iceland Kalt Einn, and now that things were calm, he'd taken a moment to make a phone call in Connall's office.

As he walked towards the kitchen again, he was overcome with desire, love, and a need to protect. His mate. His hands shook as he ran them through his hair. He could feel her heartbeat, steady and strong, her pulse slightly elevated, and he closed his eyes and took a deep breath.

Jesska watched him with a strange expression as he walked through the kitchen. "You okay?" she asked.

"My mate is close."

"Seriously?"

He nodded and headed out of the room, Jesska following. He stopped. She was here. In front of him and, admittedly, he was a little taken aback by her beauty. She had a head full of glorious red curls, porcelain skin, and a smattering of freckles across her nose. Her gray eyes widened when she caught sight of him and her cheeks pinked as she gasped. She was with a dark-haired woman, but that was all Gunnar noticed as he stared at his mate.

Grace MacMillan, Max's mate, turned to Jesska and Gunnar. "Gunnar, Jess, this is Kenna and Gillian. Payton's sisters."

Gunnar took hold of Kenna's hand, her skin soft and the connection instant. Good lord, she was beautiful. He lifted her hand and kissed her palm gently, drawing in her scent... jasmine.

She gave him a shy smile. "Hold that thought, love. I have to see to my sister, but then you and I can talk."

Gunnar stared at her and nodded, releasing her hand after he'd kissed her palm once more. He understood. Payton Gunnach was in labor upstairs with her first child and he knew she took precedence right now, but he couldn't help but be disappointed that he couldn't focus on Kenna immediately.

He wished one of them was an empath. If so, they could communicate telepathically, but until they were bound, they'd have to speak the old-fashioned way.

Since he knew she'd be a while, he texted his brothers and then took some time to ring the hotel he was currently staying at and make some plans. His bonding night was going to be one never to be forgotten.

* * *

A very healthy Killian James arrived with a feisty bellow, weighing in at eleven pounds eleven ounces and measuring twenty-four inches long.

Kenna kissed her sister and brother-in-law and then took a minute to freshen up before heading downstairs. Gillian intercepted her and pulled her into one of the guest rooms. "Are you ready for this?"

Kenna smiled. "Aye."

"Do you have any questions?"

"No, love. I'm good. He's my mate, he'll guide me."

"What if he's an arse?" Gillian asked.

Kenna laughed. "I highly doubt he's an arse."

"He's a prince, Kenna. He probably has entitlement issues."

"I don't get that vibe from him, Gillie. I'm sure he's fine."

"Maybe. But Max is an arse. Grace had to deal with him, so are you prepared to deal with Gunnar if he's an arse?"

"Why do you keep saying 'arse'?"

"Because it's a great word, but that's not the point. I'm being serious right now, sis. Are you sure you're ready?"

"Aye. And I get it. Max was difficult—"

"An arse," Gillian corrected.

"*Difficult*," Kenna said, and then giggled. "However, with Grace, his sharp edges are rounded a bit. She softens him, so I'm confident that if Gunnar is also *difficult*, I'll do the same with him. I love that you're worried, Gillie, but I'm good."

Gillian hugged her. "I can't wait to get to know him."

"Me neither, but you have to let me go so I can."

Gillian gave her one last squeeze and then released her. "Go, sweet sister. Get your bond on."

Kenna let out a sniggle. "Never say that again."

"No? I thought I might trademark it."

"Well, if you can, more power to you. Don't wait up."

Kenna headed downstairs.

Gunnar appeared before she got to the bottom step and she couldn't get over how unbelievably gorgeous he was. He had dark blond hair and deep blue eyes that crinkled at the corners when he smiled. He was everything she'd dreamed of in her mate and then some.

He wore tailored trousers and a matching jacket that appeared to have been made for him, along with a crisp, white shirt, open at the throat.

"Hi," he whispered.

She smiled, feeling a blush forming on her cheeks. "Hi."

He reached out his hand and she took it, her heart racing as he lowered his mouth to hers. She fisted her free hand in his shirt to stay upright and sighed against his lips. "Wow."

"Já, elskan. Wow." Gunnar smiled, squeezing her hand. "Are you ready now?"

She studied him for several seconds. She knew, ultimately, what he was asking and could tell he was giving her time to think. Was she ready to be bound now? Without speaking to him further or getting to know him? She'd never really thought about it until she'd watched Max and Niall go through the process with their mates. Cauld Anes typically met and bonded right away, but she'd seen how the Fallen Crown boys had had to woo their human mates, and admittedly, she wanted a little bit of that as well.

"I wish I could read your mind," he lamented.

"You'll be able to soon enough."

"Which has you hesitating."

"Not hesitating, per se," she whispered.

His thumb floated over her knuckles. "How about we go somewhere and talk? Just talk."

"I'd love that," she admitted. She was suddenly nervous. She knew he was hers, felt it in her soul, but she'd been alone a long time, and now her loneliness would be over...yet, it was change, and she was never good with change.

Gunnar lifted her hand to his lips, kissing her palm. "Come."

She grabbed her purse and followed him out of the house and to the awaiting car.

CHAPTER THREE

GUNNAR'S DRIVER WAITED by the car door, but Gunnar shook his head and held the door for Kenna instead. She smiled as she slid into the backseat, and Gunnar closed her in before speaking with his driver and then climbing in beside her.

"Are you hungry?" he asked.

"Starved."

"If we were at home, I could impress you with my knowledge of local restaurants," Gunnar said. "But I'm at a loss here in Edinburgh."

"You know you don't have to impress me. You have me. It's kind of a foregone conclusion."

Gunnar kissed her fingers. "I won't ever take that for granted, Kenna."

Kenna blushed. "That's unbelievably sweet, Gunnar."

"But no less true, sweetheart."

She squeezed his hand, a little overcome with emotion. She'd been raised to understand it, but hadn't really been prepared for the depth of it. Could someone really prepare you for what you'd feel when you met the man you were destined for? Before Gunnar, she would have said, "Yes." Now, however, she realized just how wrong she would have been. "Do you live close to Kaspar?"

He shook his head. "I live in Reykjavík."

"I love Reykjavík. I can't wait to see it through your eyes." She smiled. "For now, though, why don't we go to Sláinte? It's one of Brodie's clubs. That way I can impress you. I happen to have a permanent invitation."

He reached for her hand. "Although you impress me just by being here, I will take you up on your suggestion."

Kenna gave Cedrik, Gunnar's driver, the address and they took off toward the club. A few minutes later, they pulled up to the exclusive restaurant and Kenna had a moment of insecurity. She'd barely put any makeup on before heading over to the Gunnachs' and hadn't done anything to tame her curls. She was stepping out into public with one of the best looking men she'd ever met and here she was looking like Merida after a battle.

Gunnar climbed out of the car and Kenna used the precious few seconds she had to add a little lip-gloss. Her door opened and she pasted on what she hoped was a sincere smile.

"What?" Gunnar asked, holding out his hand. "And don't say 'nothing.'"

She sighed. "I'm just a bit of a mess. I didn't think of that before I suggested Sláinte."

Gunnar leaned in with a smile. "You're beautiful, Kenna. You could be wearing a housecoat and you'd still be the most beautiful woman in the club."

"You've never been in this club...obviously."

"Kenna," he admonished gently. "You're beautiful. It's not an opinion, it's a fact. So, I'd like you to stop acting as though you're not."

Kenna rolled her eyes. "I feel we're going to have arguments on this subject a lot."

"No arguments, elskan, as you'll do as I say at all times."

Kenna burst out laughing. "Bloody hell, love, does that typically work on the people you know?"

"Most of the time, já."

"Well, you've met your match then."

"And you have no idea how happy I am that I have."

She grinned as she slid her hand into his and climbed out of the car. Gunnar laid his hand on her lower back as they headed inside. Paige Smithers was working tonight and gave Kenna a big smile. "Ms. McFadden, what a lovely surprise. Were we expecting you?"

Paige was one of the youngest maître d's in the country. Her mother was Japanese and her father was British and she looked a little like Lucy Liu. She was stunning.

"No, Paige. I'm sorry. It was a last minute thing. I hope it's not an inconvenience."

"Not at all. I'll be with you in a moment."

Kenna felt herself leaning into Gunnar as he wrapped an arm around her waist. Paige returned within minutes and grabbed two menus. "Right this way."

Gunnar kept their connection as they followed Paige to one of the more private tables.

"Is this acceptable?" Paige asked.

"It's perfect, Paige, thank you," Kenna said, and sat down as Gunnar held the chair for her.

Once he took his seat, Paige handed them their menus and then left them alone. Gunnar smiled. "You have some clout here, hmm?"

Kenna grinned. "It helps when your brother-in-law owns the place."

"Perhaps."

"You disagree?"

"I think it's a direct result of who you are." He set his menu down. "People respect you. They don't move mountains because your brother-in-law owns the place, Kenna. They do it because they like you."

Kenna raised an eyebrow. "Really?"

He nodded. "Look around you, sweetheart. The place is packed."

"It's always packed."

"And yet, we got a prime table without a reservation."

She took a minute to take in her surroundings, but dismissed his observations. She had connections to important people, which made other people take notice.

Gunnar reached for her hand, squeezing it. "Don't dismiss my words so quickly, elskan."

"How...I mean, I wasn't..." her argument trailed off.

He chuckled. "Nice try."

She sighed, unable to stop a smile. "How did you know?"

Gunnar shrugged. "Mate-dar."

Kenna burst out laughing, covering her mouth with her free hand. "Where did you hear that?"

"It's something new I'm trying out. Americans seem to put 'dar' at the end of a lot of words, and it seemed appropriate."

"I love it."

He squeezed her hand again and they went back to their menus. Their server arrived, took their orders, and returned with the wine Gunnar had chosen. After he approved it, she poured them each a glass and left them again.

"I have a proposition," Gunnar said.

"Oh?"

"I'd like to court you."

Kenna set her glass down. "I'm sorry?"

"We are so programmed to be bound as soon as we find each other, there's no time to get to know one another."

"We'll know everything we need to once we're bound, right?" she countered.

"Já, and I can't wait, but I wonder if sometimes the whole process is rushed a little."

Kenna cocked her head. "Are you saying this for me?"

"Partly."

"Do you want to wait?"

In that moment, she didn't. She still wanted to be wooed, but perhaps after they were bound. "No."

"Well, neither do I."

"I want you to feel safe."

She smiled. "I do feel safe."

"I'm glad, elskan."

Their food arrived and Kenna took a bite, sighing in delight as she chewed her filet. "I swear this new chef puts crack in his steak."

Gunnar grinned. "Now I'm wishing I'd ordered the steak."

"Want a bite?"

"Yes, please."

She cut off a piece and fed it to him, her heart skipping a beat as his mouth wrapped around the fork. Good lord, he was sexy.

"You're right. That's amazing," he said.

"Tell me about life in Iceland," she said as they continued to eat. "Do you have a job or are you busy being royal?"

"Ah, so you know something about me then."

Kenna nodded. "Sort of. I know your brother's the king...the real king, and I know that your other brother Ari tried to hurt Pepper." She dropped her gaze, unable to meet his eyes.

He squeezed her hand and she glanced at him. "He didn't try to hurt her, Kenna. He was misguided in his approach with his daughter, granted, but he had no intention of harming her."

She scowled. "*She* felt she was in danger."

"And he's sorry for that." He sighed. "I'm not condoning what he did, but he would have never harmed her."

Kenna nodded. There wasn't really anything she could say. She hadn't been there and had heard the story somewhat secondhand, so she had to take Gunnar's word for it.

"He really wouldn't." He studied her with a gentle expression. "Ari's passionate...he's an artist at heart and he was trying to find his mate and children. I'm not sure I would have acted any better had I been in his shoes, especially now that I know who you are, so I must give him the benefit of the doubt."

"I understand. I suppose I tend to get a little protective of my friends at times and can take up offenses that aren't mine. But I do hear what you're saying."

"I love that you're loyal, Kenna. It's a wonderful quality."

"Thank you." She sipped her wine. "So, back to the original question of what you do with your day, other than being royal."

Gunnar chuckled. "I have always had an affinity with horses, so I fell into a natural trainer role. My grandparents brought several with them when they immigrated to Iceland in the ninth century. I breed and train them, as well as working with all kinds of animal rescue and rehabilitation. We hold great pride for our horses, but I do wish we had something else. I love Friesians and Arabians, but Iceland won't import them."

"Why not?"

"To keep ours from contracting diseases. We don't import any other horse, and if an Icelandic horse leaves the country it can never return."

"Really?"

"Já," he said as he laid his napkin on his lap.

"What about something like the Olympics?"

"We can compete, of course, but the horse cannot return."

Kenna let out a quiet whistle. "That would stink if you've got a bond with your horse and have to leave it wherever you compete."

"It is." He gave her a sad smile. "It's why we rarely do international competitions."

"I bet," she said. "Do you live close to your brothers?"

He shook his head. "I live in Reykjavík, although I return home a few times a year. Christmas is typically there."

"I love Reykjavík. My brother, Nevin, lives there with his mate and children."

"Really?"

She nodded. "Angus, Gillian, and I try to go every year, and of course, Fallen Crown plays there as often as they can."

"How long have you worked for them?"

"Coming up on fifty years, but it started as more of a secretary role in the beginning. Organizing signed photos and such. In the '80s they took off, and I've been managing their tours since 1990."

"And is it something you'd like to continue to do?"

"Honestly? I don't know," she admitted. "It's just something I've always done. But Max's mate is doing a great job, so there's no reason I couldn't leave the position. I have a year off for now, so I don't have to make any quick decisions."

"That works in my favor, then."

"Aye, I suppose it does." She smiled. "Do you have an opinion?"

"Not at this time. I like that we have a year to settle in, so we can talk about it in a few months. I can live anywhere, Kenna. I'm not bound to Iceland."

"So we could live here?"

"If Edinburgh's your desire, yes."

"Can we live in Iceland for a little while and then decide?"

"Já, elskan. Of course."

She grinned. "I'm excited."

"I am as well," Gunnar said with a nod.

Kenna sat back in her seat and cocked her head. "It's strange that with the amount of times I've been to Iceland, I didn't feel you."

"I agree, but I do travel, so it's possible we've been like ships passing."

"Still kind of irksome," she lamented. "I could have met you sooner."

"I know, sweetheart." He squeezed her hand again. "Tell me about your family."

"There are hundreds of us."

He nearly choked on his wine. "Hundreds?"

"Seven. There are seven."

Gunnar laughed. "You had me worried."

"My mother passed away a while ago now, so I have full siblings and half siblings. Angus is the oldest and he's mated to Kade's sister, Fiona. Nevin, then Gillian, and me. My father married a horrible lady, Phyllis, and she has Annis, Aidan, and Payton."

"Why was Phyllis a horrible lady?"

"Oh, no real reason," Kenna said. "Just a little plot to overthrow Kade."

Kenna's stepmother had concocted a grand plan to bring down the Cauld Ane king and establish her place in the royal family, however, she'd been unsuccessful.

"She masterminded the plot?"

Kenna nodded. "And she was horribly abusive to Payton. You have to understand something about Payton. She's our favorite. We'll all admit it, it doesn't take away from how much we love each other, but ultimately, she's all of our favorites."

"What happened to Phyllis?"

"She and Annis, who was part of the plot with her mate, were exiled to Pohnpei."

"Appropriate."

Kenna sighed. "I suppose so."

"You don't agree?"

"It's just hard when it's your own family, you know? What they did was horrible, and I agree they should be punished, it's just hard to know your sister is being sent to her death."

Gunnar gave her a gentle smile. "Yes, I can see that being difficult."

Their server returned to take their plates and Gunnar asked for the check.

"Where are we going after this?" Kenna asked, setting her napkin on the table.

"I have a few things set up at the hotel, if that's acceptable."

She nodded. "Can we swing by my place first so I can pack a bag, please?"

"Of course."

Gunnar paid the check and then followed Kenna out to the car.

CHAPTER FOUR

K ENNA UNLOCKED THE front door and led Gunnar inside. "Make yourself at home, love. I won't be long."

Before she could head upstairs to her room, however, he pulled her into his arms and kissed her, then settled his forehead against hers. "I needed something to tide me over."

Kenna giggled, stroking his cheek. "One more?"

He grinned and obliged. Kenna broke the kiss and rushed up to her room, stalling when she saw a gift bag on her bed. Opening the card, she smiled.

I hope you have the sense to come home and get your things before you go somewhere magical for your bonding. Take this with you and wow him. Love you, sis. G.

Peeking inside she found a sexy, white, sheer nightie, complete with matching underwear, and felt a blush cover her cheeks.

She grabbed her overnight duffel, threw in a couple changes of clothes and the new nightie, and then headed to the bathroom for makeup and such. She was quite proud of herself, only taking ten minutes to grab everything she needed.

Arriving downstairs, she found Gunnar texting madly on his phone. He glanced up and smiled before sliding the phone in his pocket. "All set?"

"Yes." She nodded towards his pocket. "Are you?"

He grinned. "That would be telling."

"What did you do?"

He put his finger to his lips. "It's a surprise."

"I love surprises."

"Good." He took her bag from her. "Come."

Kenna locked the house up and followed Gunnar to the car. He waited for her to climb inside before following. He took her hand as the driver pulled away from the curb, and Kenna was pleasantly surprised when they pulled up to the Balmoral.

"I love this place," she said.

"It's my first time here," Gunnar admitted. "But they've been really attentive so far."

Kenna grinned. "Well, if they give us any grief, I know a guy."

Gunnar laughed. "I bet you do."

A bellboy met them as they climbed out of the car and took Kenna's bag from the driver. "Welcome back, Mr. Baldursson."

"Thank you," Gunnar said, laying his hand on Kenna's lower back.

Kenna stayed connected to Gunnar as the bellboy led them to the elevator and up to their suite. Gunnar wrapped an arm around Kenna as they walked down the hall and she bit the inside of her cheek to keep from squeaking out loud. The bellboy led them inside and placed the bag in the bedroom. Gunnar tipped him and he went on his way.

"You have the Scone & Crombie Suite!" Kenna finally squeaked in glee, throwing her arms around his neck. "I love this room."

He wrapped his arms around her, pulling her close. "I did hear that somewhere."

"You did?"

"I have a small confession." Gunnar chuckled, releasing her. "Grace organized it. She and I had a little chat after you left me to tend to your sister. That was her on the phone confirming everything."

"Oh, I love that girl!"

"She feels the same about you." He took her hand and led her into the bedroom. The bed had rose petals fashioned in a heart and in the corner a bottle of champagne sat chilling next to two glasses and a plate with some kind of confection.

"Is that salted caramel?" she asked.

"Já, elskan. Grace said it's your favorite."

"It *is* my favorite. As is the Dom Perignon." She wrapped her arms around his waist and sighed. "Thank you, love. Everything's perfect."

He kissed the top of her head and held her for a few minutes before releasing her. "I'll leave you to change."

She smiled up at him. "Okay."

Gunnar left the bedroom and Kenna grabbed her new lingerie and headed into the bathroom. She pushed away her nerves once she studied herself in the mirror. Gillian had picked the absolute perfect outfit for her. It gave her a little more on top and helped to round out her hips a little. She had a lithe, athletic figure that she'd never hated, necessarily, but she sometimes wished she had a little more curve. She took a deep breath and headed back into the bedroom. "I'm ready," she called.

Gunnar walked back in and Kenna licked her lips. He wore a loose pair of pajama pants, black, and nothing else. "Kenna," he whispered. "You are beautiful."

She grinned. "You are too."

His chest was muscular and sprinkled with freckles that Kenna wanted to play connect the dots with. He held his arms out and she gripped them just below his elbows. He wrapped his hands around her arms as well and smiled. "Ready?"

"Yes."

"Hold on tight," Gunnar directed, and then kissed her gently.

"Aye, love." She'd been warned that once the final bonding word was spoken, she'd feel like fainting.

"*Ég gef þér allt sem ég er, allt sem ég vil vera og allt sem ég get verið.*"

"*Ég gef þér allt sem ég er, allt sem ég vil vera og allt sem ég get verið,*" Kenna said, feeling her knees weaken. Even though she was prepared for it, she still gripped his arms harder.

"I've got you." Gunnar grinned and continued, "*Ég er þinn að eilífu. Ég er þinn að eilífu. Eining okkar mun aldrei bresta.*"

"*Ég er þinn að eilífu. Ég er þinn að eilífu. Eining okkar mun aldrei bresta.*" Kenna took a deep breath as Gunnar wrapped an arm around her waist to steady her.

"*Ást mín er alger.*"

"Ást mín er alger." She smiled. "Together."

"Já."

In unison, they spoke, "Ég gef þér allt sem ég er, allt sem ég vil vera og allt sem ég get verið. Ég er þinn að eilífu. Ég er þinn að eilífu. Eining okkar mun aldrei bresta. Ást mín er alger"

As she finished the last line of their bonding words, Kenna thought them to herself in English and sighed. *I give you everything I am, all I want to be and all I can be. I'm yours forever. Our bond will never be broken. My love is absolute.*

"I love you."

"I love you too," Gunnar whispered, and lifted her from her feet and carried her to the bed.

An hour later, Kenna lay across Gunnar's chest trying to catch her breath. "Wow."

Gunnar chuckled. "Yes, exactly. Wow."

"I was expecting that to be bad."

"Why?" he demanded.

"I was told the first time is *always* bad."

"Who told you that?"

"My mother," she admitted.

"Well, I'm sad for your mother."

She wrinkled her nose. "I don't want to talk about my mother while I'm lying over your sexy, naked body."

Gunnar grinned. "Fair enough."

She kissed his chest before settling her chin on her hands. "Do you want to try?"

He raised an eyebrow. *I don't know, do you?*

"It worked!" *I mean, it worked!*

He chuckled. *This is going to be fun.*

Aye, love, 'tis. She raised an eyebrow. "What are your gifts...normally?"

"The usual ones, suggestion, telekinesis—"

"*Usual* ones?" She sat up a little. "I don't have telekinesis."

"You don't?"

She shook her head.

"What do you have?" he asked.

"Psycometry and suggestion, but my gift of suggestion isn't as strong as say, Max's."

"Hmm. I wonder why that is?"

She shrugged. "I have no idea, but I love that I'm going to be able to move things with my mind."

Gunnar grinned. "We'll practice after we shower."

"Can we practice *in* the shower?"

"Absolutely."

Kenna slid off the bed and Gunnar followed. In the end, the tub beckoned and they skipped the shower, opting for making love in the tub. The emotions Kenna was experiencing couldn't be put into words, so she let them swamp her, grateful she and Gunnar hadn't waited any longer to be bound. Her love was absolute and she knew he felt the same.

CHAPTER FIVE

THE NEXT MORNING, Kenna led Gunnar out of the hotel, squeezing his hand as she grinned up at him. "I can't wait for you to meet Angus and Fiona. My brother can be a bit of a bear at times, but Fiona's lovely. She's done loads of research about all of us, so I know she'll want to ply you with questions. We've lost so much information in the past years, and we're finding out much of what we were told was inaccurate at best."

Gunnar smiled. "She must visit our home, then. Everything's archived there. Information as far back as just after the crucifixion of Christ."

"Shut up, really?"

"Já. Kaspar even has some Aramaic texts and records. I don't know where they came from, but they're quite remarkable to see."

"Wow, that sounds amaz—"

Before she could finish her thought, a sharp pain shot through her side and she fell to the ground.

"Kenna!" Gunnar yelled, and dropped beside her as people screamed and ran for cover. "Ansans! Cedrik!"

"I'm on it, highness," Cedrik bellowed as he rushed past them and into the crowd.

"Kenna?" Gunnar whispered, checking her body to find the bullet wound.

"I can't breathe," she rasped.

"I know, baby. It's okay. I've got you." He placed his palm over her chest and leaned over her for privacy as he worked to heal her. *Work with me, Kenna.*

It hurts.

I know, sweetheart, but it won't hurt for long. Focus.

What happened?

You've been shot.

"What?" she squeaked.

"Shh, Kenna," Gunnar admonished. "I need you to focus."

She closed her eyes and together they moved the bullet from her body and healed the lung it had pierced. As she felt her lung expand again, she gulped in as much air as she could.

"Slowly, sweetheart, you don't want to hyperventilate."

She nodded and licked her lips.

"Feel good enough to get up?" he asked.

"Aye, love," she said. "I'm fine."

Gunnar had used his power of suggestion to keep the crowds away and he pulled her to her feet without anyone questioning her ability to walk after being shot in the chest.

Kenna scowled down at her bloody shirt. "Bloody hell. I loved this top."

"We can buy you another top, sweetheart." He slid out of his button-up, leaving him in a tight T-shirt, and handed it to her. "Put this on over it and we'll head back to the room to change."

She nodded and did as he instructed. Before Gunnar could usher her back inside, however, the angry voice of Donnall Mann bellowed, "Where the hell is my wife?"

Kenna gasped as he moved to strike her, but she shouldn't have been concerned. Cedrik had him by the throat and up against the wall of the hotel within seconds, Donnall's once concealed gun now on the ground beside him.

Gunnar took Donnall from Cedrik and slammed his head against the brick.

Don't kill him, Gunnar.

"Kenna, call the police," Gunnar said, ignoring her suggestion.

She nodded and pulled out her cell phone, dialing the officer who'd helped with Claire. "Officer Tarver? Hi, this is Kenna McFadden, ah, I've got a bit of a situation down here at the Balmoral. Claire Mann's husband just attacked me. Aye, he's detained right now. My ma—husband has him." She bit her lip and grimaced at her near mis-speak. "Right. Yes, okay. Thank you." She hung up and slid her phone back in her pocket. "He'll be here in twenty minutes."

"I shot you," Donnall rasped. "I saw you go down."

"I don't understand how you even found me," Kenna said.

"I followed you, you ignorant cow."

I can't believe I was so stupid not to notice.

You're not stupid, sweetheart.

She frowned up at Gunnar.

"Let Cedrik take you up to the room, sweetheart," he suggested. "You can change and I'll take care of him until the police arrive."

"I don't think I should leave you."

Gunnar chuckled. "I think it would be best that you are cleaned up and in something a little less bloody before they arrive."

"Right, good idea," she said.

He smiled gently. "I'll sort out our story."

"I won't be long." She rushed back inside and up to their room, Cedrik rushing ahead to shield her if need be. No one bothered her, so she had a clear shot into their suite. After Cedrik checked the room, he left her alone and Kenna shoved her bloody clothes into a plastic bag. Tying the bag and hiding it in her suitcase, she took a quick shower and got dressed. She remembered to grab a new shirt for Gunnar and arrived in the lobby just before the officer and his partner walked inside.

"Are you injured, Ms. McFadden?" Officer Tarver asked.

I have the man in the security office. It's right next to the concierge desk.

"No, I'm fine. Just a little shaken."

"Where is Mr. Mann?"

"Back this way." Kenna led the officers into the private area where Gunnar had Donnall controlled for the moment.

Kenna slid into Gunnar's arms as one of the officer's cuffed Donnall and led him away. Officer Tarver took Kenna and Gunnar's statements and then left them with a promise to follow up the next day.

"How about we postpone lunch with your brother and his family, sweetheart?" Gunnar asked as they walked back into their suite.

Kenna shook her head. "Do you mind if we don't? I'd really like to see them."

He cupped her face and frowned. "Baby, I need to know you're okay."

"I will be." She bit back tears as the fright finally took hold. "I just need a distraction and they're a really good distraction."

He pulled her close and kissed the top of her head. "If I think you need to be away from the chaos, elskan, we're leaving."

Kenna couldn't help but smile as she closed her eyes and burrowed into his chest. "I'm good with that."

Gunnar tipped her head back and kissed her gently. "You're calming."

She nodded. "Aye, love. I'm okay."

He stroked her cheek and then gave her a nod. "The rule still stands."

Kenna chuckled. "I know, love."

He released her, buttoned up his clean shirt, and then led her out of the hotel.

* * *

One week later...

Reykjavík, Iceland

"Gunnar, it's magnificent," Kenna breathed out as she walked into his flat.

They had arrived barely half an hour ago from the private airstrip in Reykjavík, and Kenna was still a little amped from their flight.

Gunnar's apartment had floor-to-ceiling windows that overlooked the Reykjavík Harbor, close to the Harpa Concert Hall. A modern kitchen opened into a great room and there were three bedrooms and three bathrooms, all on one floor.

"It's small, but it serves my purposes."

Kenna faced him. "If you think this is small, love, I wonder what you consider big."

"You may have a point." He grinned and pulled her close. "I don't have staff here full time, but if you feel you need something, let me know."

"I don't need staff, Gunnar. I've been on the road most of the past twenty years, so being in one spot for more than a month is a treat. I also love to cook, so cooking in such a beautiful space will be a luxury I haven't had before."

He stroked her cheek. "Are you always this agreeable?"

She laughed. "Yes?"

"A question, hmm? Not a definitive statement."

"That's because my siblings would probably argue the 'yes.'"

"They wouldn't in front of me."

"Oh, you might be surprised," she countered.

He smiled. "I wonder what I did to deserve you."

"Because I'm agreeable?"

"Because you're perfect. I think I must have rescued puppies from burning buildings in a past life to have deserved you."

Kenna settled her cheek on his chest and sighed. "I'm not perfect, but I'm glad I'm creating an illusion...at least for a little while."

"Are you tired?"

"I'm a little antsy actually, but I know I'm going to crash anytime. I always do after flying."

"We have a lovely big tub if you want to decompress a bit," he said. "Tomorrow we'll explore."

"Sounds amazing." She glanced up at him. "Are you joining me in the tub?"

"What a silly question," he said. "Of *course* I'm joining you in the tub. But before that I'll pour wine."

Kenna grinned and followed him into the kitchen. While he poured two glasses of Merlot, she explored the kitchen. "I'm in love."

"Aw, thank you, elskan."

"With this room," she clarified.

"Pots and pans over your mate. I see how it is."

Kenna shook her head. "You'll be changing your tune once you taste what I make in those pots and pans."

"I would never choose pots and pans over you, sweetheart." He laid his palm over his heart. "I love you *that* much.

She giggled. "You're good, baby."

"Thank you." He handed her a glass of wine. "Now, the bags are here, so we'll relax and then tomorrow you'll see the city through my eyes and we'll visit your family."

"Perfect," she said and, once he locked up, she followed him to the master bedroom.

CHAPTER SIX

THE NEXT MORNING, Kenna was awakened with a scruffy kiss and she sighed as Gunnar rolled her to face him. "*Góðan daginn.*"

"Morning." She smiled sleepily and yawned, closing her eyes again. "What time is it?"

"Almost nine."

She groaned, peering up at him through one eye. "Why are you waking me so early, you evil man?"

"Because I made breakfast."

"You did?" she asked.

"Yes. I didn't know if you were a breakfast in bed person or not, so I'm waking you to find out."

Kenna giggled. "I'm a sleep-in-until-noon person, eliminating the need for questions about breakfast in bed."

"So, lunch in bed?"

"Sleep, reading, and sex in bed. No food," she said, definitively.

"Mmm, I'm all for sex in bed."

She slid her hands in his hair. "Didn't you say you already *made* breakfast?"

"Do coffee and toast count?"

"Good lord, you're lucky you're cute."

He grinned, leaning down to kiss her. Breakfast was forgotten as she was fully awakened in a much nicer way, then she joined Gunnar for breakfast on the balcony.

The water was still and the sun glistened over it, making it look like glass. "So Reykjavík Harbor sits where, exactly?"

"Faxaflói," he said.

"Does that lead out to the Atlantic?" Kenna asked.

"Eventually."

"You can see for miles," she breathed out.

"I know. As soon as I toured this flat, I knew I had to have it."

She smiled. "I don't think I need to go back to Scotland."

Gunnar chuckled. "You might change your mind when we have babies. You may want your sisters close."

"Hmm, yes, babies. I didn't think about bairns." She turned her head to look at him. "How many do you want?"

"How many do you want to give me?"

"Two?"

He nodded. "Two is perfect."

She turned back to the water. "You're right, I probably *will* want to be close to my family when we have kids," she conceded.

"Why don't we buy a place in Edinburgh? My business and charity interests can be managed from anywhere, so anytime you feel homesick, we'll head to Scotland, and whenever we want to be here, we'll be here."

She sighed. "I love you."

"I love you too."

"How close are Ari and Megan?"

"They live about fifteen minutes away. They'll be home from Charlotte's in a few days, so we'll have them over if you want to."

"I'd love to," Kenna said. "Especially if I can cook."

"You can most definitely cook, elskan." Gunnar grinned, rising to his feet so he could lean over her. "Are you ready to explore?"

"Yes! I can't wait."

He took her cup from her and led her back into the house. Pulling out his phone, he fired off a text and slid the phone into his pocket. "The car is here. We'll start in the middle of the city and go from there. I have a lunch reservation for us at Grillmarkadurinn. It's one of my favorite restaurants, so now it's my turn to impress you."

"Well, now I'm hungry all over again," Kenna complained, and wrapped her arms around his waist.

He patted her bottom, leaning down to kiss her. "Don't worry, elskan. I *will* feed you."

She bit her lip. "Now I'm hungry in a different way."

Gunnar dropped his head back with a groan. "Baby, you're killing me."

Kenna giggled. "Am I too much for you already?"

"We could skip the tour of the city," he said. "Just head to lunch directly from here."

She licked her lips. "We could also tour the city *after* lunch."

Gunnar lifted her off her feet and she wrapped her legs around his waist. "That's a great idea."

Kenna slid her fingers through his hair as he carried her back to the bedroom. "Shouldn't you tell Cedrik we're going to be late?"

"Priorities, elskan. I plan to get you naked first."

"Well, hurry up, then."

Gunnar laughed and did as he was told.

* * *

Two hours later, Kenna followed Gunnar out of the apartment and down to the car. They were fifteen minutes late for their reservation, but apparently, it wasn't a problem for the popular restaurant.

"I hate being late," she confessed as they took their seats.

The server handed them their menus and then walked away.

"We're fine, sweetheart. I know the chef."

"That's not really the point," she countered.

He peeked at her over the menu before laying it down. "This really bothers you."

"Yes, I suppose it does," she admitted. "I've spent a big chunk of my life organizing four very strong-willed men, along with a crew of a hundred, making sure they got where they needed to be, on time. It's ingrained in me that if one person is late, it can have frustrating and sometimes expensive consequences." She sighed. "Perhaps I'm over-reacting."

"Or perhaps you're just being sensitive to people. That's something kind, sweetheart. You can help me with this area, I'm sure of it."

"I didn't mean to make you feel bad."

"You didn't." He reached out and took her hand. "Am I concerned that being fifteen minutes late to a restaurant will have dire consequences? No. Mostly, because I know Birgir, and he has always said I have an open invitation to come whenever I please. He and I went to school together, so we've known each other for a long time. However, is it a rule that I could follow a little more closely in other areas? Yes."

"Thank you."

He grinned. "Would you like me to order for you?"

"I think I'm okay." She glanced over the menu. "My Icelandic is better than I remember."

Gunnar chuckled. "Having a brother living here probably helps."

"Aye, it does. Although, when he swears, he usually reverts to Gaelic."

"Good to know."

The smiling server returned with glasses of water and asked, "*Eruð þið tilbúin að panta?*" (Are you ready to order?)

"*Skötusel, takk,*" Kenna said. (Monkfish, please)

Gunnar laid the menu down and glanced up at the server. "*Grillað lamba prime, takk.*" (Grilled prime of lamb.)

He ordered wine for each of them as well, and then the server took their menus and left them.

Kenna took a sip of her water and smiled. "I'm glad we're walking the city after this, because I have a feeling I'm going to be stuffed."

"The food here is excellent, so you are correct in that assessment." He smoothed his napkin over his knee. "What time are we expected tonight?"

"Six," Kenna said. "I have little gifts for the kids, but I'd like to stop and grab some wine before we go, if that's okay."

"No. We don't buy wine here," he joked.

Kenna giggled. "Then we're definitely living in Scotland full time."

Gunnar grinned. "On the living and visiting subject, Kaspar has asked if we want to join them early December and stay until after the New Year. We could also ask them here."

"Right, Christmas at your brother's?"

"Já. Is there a problem?"

She bit her lip. "I've just never been away from my family at Christmastime. Generally, if we can't go to Nevin, he comes to us. Our family's always together for the holidays."

"How would they feel about joining everyone at Kaspar's? Their house is big enough and I know we would enjoy it."

"I'll ask Nevin tonight and then we can work on the rest of the family. Angus is bound to Fiona now, so he may stay with the Gunnachs'. Gillian is usually quite flexible." She didn't know what to do about Payton and Brodie. She couldn't imagine spending a holiday without her youngest sister.

"Sweetheart, we can stay with your family instead. I know you're especially close with Payton, so whatever you want to do is fine."

She gave him a shy smile. "I forget that you can read my mind."

"I don't know why you didn't feel you could tell me that...out loud."

"Because I'm a people pleaser."

Gunnar smiled. "Well, now it's time for people to please you."

"I'm sure it will all work out."

"Yes, it will...once you tell me what you want to do."

"I'll have to think about it."

"Fair enough." He reached for her hand again. "I love you, Kenna."

"I love you too."

The server arrived with their food and they focused on the culinary delights that had been placed in front of them before heading out to stroll through the city.

They'd just turned down Laugavegur when Gunnar guided Kenna into a lovely little boutique jewelry store and up to the counter. An elderly man gave Gunnar a huge smile and clapped his hands. "*Herra Baldursson, velkomin.*"

"Herra Fjólarsson," Gunnar said, and switched to English. "This is my wife, Kenna."

"Lovely to meet you," he said.

"It's lovely to meet you too."

"Do you have the rings?" Gunnar asked.

"Yes, yes. I'll be just a moment."

He scurried into the back room and Kenna squeezed Gunnar's hand. "What's going on?"

"My wife needs a wedding ring."

She bounced a little as she grinned up at him. "Yes, yes, she does. But you need one as well."

"We're getting them now." He wrapped his arms around her and kissed her nose. "Plus I have a little surprise for you."

"I thought the wedding rings were the surprise."

"Here we are," Mr. Fjólarsson said as he returned. He settled a black velvet tray on the counter and Kenna gasped at the rings on display.

"Pick whichever one you like," Gunnar said. "And if these aren't to your taste, we'll order whatever you want."

Kenna clasped her fingers at her chest and leaned in to get a closer look. She had been alive long enough to amass a small fortune of her own, but even so, she was still Scottish and tended to fall on the frugal side. These rings were a beautiful gluttony of diamonds. Some with emeralds, some with sapphires, but she was drawn to one that was just diamonds. The white gold band was designed with intricately woven filigree and tiny diamonds up the sides. A huge princess cut diamond sat proudly in the middle and Kenna bit her lip as she pointed to it. "May I try that one, please?"

"Yes, yes, of course." Mr. Fjólarsson seemed particularly excited by her choice as he slid it on her finger. "Exquisite."

"It fits perfectly," Kenna said as she held it up. "I love it."

"You have the matching bands?" Gunnar prompted.

"Já. Right here." Mr. Fjólarsson opened the cabinet in front of them and pulled out several styles.

"I get to pick this one," Gunnar said.

"Oh, really?" Kenna raised an eyebrow.

He chuckled. "I have a feeling you will be careful in your spending."

"Don't talk to me like you know me," she retorted.

With a huge grin, Gunnar picked the diamond encrusted band that matched her engagement ring, along with a plain white gold one, identical to the man's larger one next to it.

"I don't need two," Kenna said.

He didn't respond as he took her hand and slid off the engagement ring. Taking the plain band, he slid it on, then the engagement ring again, then the diamond band, lifting her hand to his lips. "I love you."

She smiled. "I love you too."

Taking Gunnar's band from the jeweler, she slid it on Gunnar's hand and kissed his fingers before releasing him and wrapping her arm around his waist.

Mr. Fjólarsson almost squealed with joy as Gunnar handed him his credit card and paid the equivalent of nearly one hundred thousand pounds. This was a very good day all around in Kenna's opinion.

They left the store, Gunnar guiding her because she couldn't keep from admiring the major bling on her hand. "I can't believe it was in my size."

"I called ahead," he admitted.

"Even still, it was fast."

"Mr. Fjólarsson has always been good to my brothers and me, so we are good to him."

She grinned up at him. "And you're good to me. I love the rings, Gunnar. Thank you."

"Believe me when I say it was my pleasure." He leaned down and kissed her gently. "Are you ready to go home and change?"

"Is it that time already?" She checked her watch. "Oh, wow, it is."

"Come." Gunnar slid his phone back in his pocket. "Cedrik will have the car waiting."

Kenna nodded and they headed to the car.

CHAPTER SEVEN

NEVIN PULLED OPEN the door with a grin and Kenna rushed into her brother's embrace. "Och, I've missed you, Nevvie."

"I've missed you too, lass. You look beautiful."

"This is why you're my favorite brother," she confessed. "You always tell me I'm pretty."

"I always speak the truth." Nevin laughed, setting her aside and reaching his hand out to Gunnar as he bowed. "Your Highness. Welcome."

"Gunnar, please. We're family now." Gunnar shook his hand. "It's nice to meet you."

"Come and meet everyone." Nevin closed the door behind them. "Clara insisted on cooking tonight, so you're in for a treat."

Kenna moved through the house with ease, knowing it almost as well as Gillian's. "Where are me wee minions? Hmmm? Why is it so quiet? Are they hiding from their auntie Kenna?" A stifled giggle sounded in the hall closet. "Oh, no. The wee laddies and lassies couldn't possibly be hiding from their auntie. She has pressies for them."

The door to the closet flew open and Mary, the tiniest dark-haired lassie, threw herself against Kenna's legs, while the pitter-patter of feet came from different parts of the house.

"Auntie," the kids all yelled in unison.

"I knew you were all here. Little devils," she said.

Clara rushed into the living room and curtsied. "Your Highness."

"Gunnar, please," he insisted again, and reached out his hand.

Clara shook it and smiled. "Gunnar. Welcome."

"What did you bring us?" Mary asked.

"Well, your new uncle has the bag. How about we meet him and then he can show you," Kenna said as she lifted her niece into her arms. Mary slid her head into Kenna's neck, blushing as she peeked at Gunnar. "This is my mate, lovelies. Gunnar."

"I'm Isaac." The sixteen-year-old shook Gunnar's hand and Gunnar handed him a CD of secret songs signed by the members of Fallen Crown. "This is so cool, Auntie. Thank you. And nice to meet you, Gunnar."

Gunnar grinned. "You too."

"This is Emma," Kenna said. "She and Mary are both a little shy. But Andrew isn't...where *is* Andrew? He's disappeared again."

"Andrew," Nevin called. "Where did you go?"

The nine-year-old ran into the room wielding a sword. "I have a sword."

Kenna bit back a laugh as he waved it in the air.

"Já. That's a big sword there, Andrew." Gunnar knelt down to his level. "Do you know how to use it?"

He shook his head. "Papa says he's going to get me lessons."

"That's a good idea," Gunnar agreed. "Then you and I can practice."

Andrew's eyes widened. "You know how to sword fight?"

"Yes. I've been in a few battles in my time. I'll show you some things."

"Okay!"

The rest of the gifts were passed out and then the kids ran off to play while the adults chatted in the kitchen.

"Would you like a beer or wine, your High...ah, Gunnar?" Clara asked.

"Wine would be great, thank you."

"I'll get it," Kenna said, and rose from the table.

Clara peeked into the oven. "Thanks, love."

Kenna poured wine for everyone but her brother who already had a beer, and then sat at the table with Gunnar again.

"I can hear you thinking," Nevin accused.

Kenna giggled. "I have always hated that ability."

"Me too, love," Clara admitted as she salted the potatoes.

"So, what's got you thinking?" Nevin prompted.

"Christmas."

"Ah. And where we're all going to be?"

Kenna nodded. "Kaspar has invited us to stay there."

"The king has offered his home?" Clara asked in reverence.

"For everyone," Gunnar said. "Including your family, if you'd like to join us."

Clara glanced at Nevin, blushed, and then focused back on the food.

"We'd be honored to join you," Nevin said.

Kenna sighed. "I thought that would be harder."

"You're newly bonded, sis," Nevin said. "We had already discussed doing what we could to be close to you this year, so it's an easy decision."

Kenna jumped out of her seat and hugged her brother around his neck. "I love you, I love you, I love you."

Nevin laughed. "Get off me, ye bampot."

Gunnar reached for her, pulling her onto his lap. "I'll take some of that."

Kenna grinned, leaning down to kiss him. "I'm happy to give you whatever you need."

Once dinner was ready, they sat down to eat and Kenna felt much more settled about future plans. She couldn't wait for Christmas and everything they would be experiencing together.

CHAPTER
EIGHT

Six months later...

KENNA WALKED TOWARD the library of Payton's home in an attempt to find her mate. She and Gunnar were visiting for a couple of weeks so that Gunnar could work with Connall's horses. It was the perfect opportunity to visit family and snuggle Killian who, at barely six months old, was the size of a small horse.

Walking into Brodie's library, she stalled to find Gunnar and Brodie, heads down, studying something on Brodie's desk.

"Here you are," Kenna said, trying to keep her irrational exasperation from her voice and failing miserably. She'd been on edge for the past week or so and not sure why.

The men looked up and Gunnar smiled, waving her over. "We're just looking at house plans."

"For who?"

"Us."

"What?" she asked as she joined them at the desk. "I thought you were just complaining about the fact we can't find anything in Edinburgh."

"But there is something here," Gunnar said, wrapping an arm around her.

Were we going to talk about this before you surprised *me?*

He raised an eyebrow, but didn't have a chance to answer because Brodie started in. "I have six acres at the edge of my property that I either need to build a home on or let go. Payton wanted to build a home on it to house family when they come...we're all growing in numbers now, and even this house can't accommodate everyone."

Kenna nodded, her irritation easing a little bit. "You don't still want to do that?"

"Not if you and Gunnar want it," Brodie said. "He's offered a more than fair price for the land and it means Payton will have you close when you come to visit. But it's up to you, Kenna. I really don't mind either way."

"We'll talk it over and let you know before we leave," Gunnar said.

Brodie nodded just as Payton walked in with Killian. "Da!" he squealed.

"There's my wee moose now," Brodie crooned, catching his son as Killian pitched forward reaching for him. "You almost took yer mum out, Kill."

"You've got that right," Payton said. "You need to stop growing, love."

Killian settled his head on Brodie's shoulder and stuck his thumb in his mouth. Payton eyed Kenna as she shrugged away from Gunnar.

"Can I borrow you for a bit, Kenna?" Payton asked.

"Aye, lass," she said, glancing up at Gunnar. *We'll talk about all of this later.*

Gunnar nodded, leaning down to kiss her gently. *What are you keeping from me?*

Nothing, why?

"Go with your sister," he said. "We'll make some decisions when you get back."

Kenna nodded and followed Payton out of the library. Payton grabbed her arm and dragged her into the bathroom.

"What are you doing?" Kenna squeaked.

Payton held up a pregnancy test. "You are going to pee on this stick."

"What, why?"

"Because you're irritable, snappy, and being an all-around bitch to your mate."

Kenna scowled as she crossed her arms. "That doesn't mean I'm pregnant."

"Pee!" Payton turned toward the door. "I won't look."

"Bloody hell, Payton, I'm no' peeing with you in the room."

Payton plugged her ears. "I won't listen either," she said in an almost shout.

Kenna let out a frustrated groan, but did as her sister ordered and set the test on the counter while she washed her hands. She tapped Payton's shoulder and Payton turned to face her again.

"Have I really been treating Gunnar that badly?"

"Aye, love you have," Payton said. "It's completely out of character for you. You don't even speak to Max like that, and he can be an arse."

Kenna dropped her face in her hands. "I'm just wee bit off at the moment."

"I know, sis." Payton leaned forward and let out a, "squee!"

Kenna gasped. "It's positive."

"Kenna?" Gunnar knocked on the bathroom door. "Are you all right?"

"I'll leave you to talk," Payton said. "Be nice."

"Och, go on with you." Kenna pushed her sister gently out of the bathroom and wrapped her arms around Gunnar's waist. "I'm so sorry."

He slid her hair away from her neck. "What are you sorry for, elskan?"

"I've been such a horrid shrew."

"Who told you that?" Gunnar chuckled. "It's not true."

She smiled up at him. "You're a horrible liar, but I love you for it."

"So, we're going to have a baby?"

Kenna grinned, nodding. "We're having a baby."

Gunnar pulled her close, kissing her gently. "I love you."

"I love you too. I'll try not to let my emotions overtake my normally sweet, agreeable self."

Gunnar burst out laughing. "Sweetheart, you've been a little on edge, but you're still sweet and agreeable."

"Not according to Payton," Kenna grumbled. "She said I'm being a bitch."

"Ansans," he hissed. "You are not."

"Thank you for that, but I need to be nicer to you."

He lifted her chin and stroked her cheek. "How about *I* decide if you need to be nicer to me? This is none of Payton's business, Kenna. You and I are a team, já?"

"Don't be mad at Payton, honey, she was on your side."

"I'm mad at no one." He tempered his annoyance with a smile. "But I also don't want you thinking you've done anything wrong. I've known something's been up with you for the past week. It's not just the edginess. Your body's also changing."

"Aye." She grimaced. "My boobs are huge."

"And this is a problem, why?" She playfully smacked his chest and Gunnar laughed. He pulled her close again and kissed her temple. "Do you want to talk about the house?"

She nodded and leaned away from him. "But later, okay? Right now I want to process the fact I'm going to be pushing a human being out of my body in less than six months. And then all the scheduling around Christmas. And then—"

He cut off her rambling by covering her mouth with his and sliding his hand into her hair. She sighed as she relaxed against him and smiled against his lips. "Low blow, Gunnar."

"You're not going to worry about any of this, sweetheart. We'll sort it out, and I know our families will help." Gunnar cupped her cheeks, settling his thumb over her lips when she started to speak. "No. You will enjoy this baby. You won't worry about details that will work themselves out. Hear me on that."

She kissed his thumb and rolled her eyes. "When did you suddenly get so bossy?"

"The second you told me about the baby."

"So you're going to be like this for the entire six months?"

"Making you relax and doing my best to take away your worries?" he countered. "Hell, yes I am."

She shivered. "Why does that make me so hot?"

Gunnar dropped his head back and laughed. "I have no idea, but I can cool you down right now if you like."

Kenna bobbed her head up and down. "Yes, please."

He grabbed her hand and led her up to their bedroom intending to soothe the desire she was swamping both of them with. However, he only managed to heat them both up again. Kenna wondered if her entire pregnancy would prove to always be this sexy.

Bíldudalur, Iceland

December...

KENNA TOOK A deep breath and pushed herself up from the airplane seat. Gunnar was up talking to the pilot and Kenna needed off this plane. They'd had a pleasant and relatively quick trip from Reykjavik, even still, Kenna couldn't wait to find a tub to soak in.

"Elskan," Gunnar admonished. "Why didn't you wait for me?"

"Because I have to pee," she whispered. "Which is all I ever need to do these days anyway."

She was five-and-a-half months pregnant with their little boy and, with less than one month to go, she was feeling anxious to get the baby out. She waddled down the aisle, grateful they were flying private so the bathroom was an *actual* bathroom. Just the thought of trying to stuff her huge body into a commercial airplane toilet made her want to hurt someone.

You're not huge.

Kenna rolled her eyes. *Humpback whales are smaller than me, Gunnar, so I disagree.*

She washed her hands and opened the door to find her mate lurking. "I'm okay, love. You don't have to follow me everywhere."

"Humor me," he said.

Gunnar was more and more protective the closer the baby came, and as much as Kenna loved him, she also felt a little crowded on occasion.

She smiled, kissing his cheek and wrapping an arm around his waist. "I'm ready."

"We have to go down the stairs, so I'll go first. Stay close."

They'd done this before. Twice. She knew the drill, but didn't comment. She knew he felt the need to say it out loud. If she were to slip going down the stairs, she'd slip into him. It's why she went first going up. All to protect her.

Kenna followed him down the stairs and into a large black SUV. Someone else handled the luggage and she grabbed a bottle of water from the middle console. Gunnar climbed into the car beside her and pulled out his phone, firing off a text to Kaspar.

"How's your breathing?" Gunnar asked.

"Good, baby, I'm just tired."

Gunnar took her hand and kissed her palm. "Are you excited?"

"Definitely." She grinned. "I'm looking forward to everyone being together this year."

"Even Ari and Kaspar?"

Kenna giggled. "I like them."

"Despite Kade's opinion of my brothers, hmm?"

She giggled. "I'm pretty sure Samantha's working on that."

"True. I don't know that I'll ever be able to thank her enough for freeing Ari. Especially since Kade's reasons for keeping him locked up were justified."

"If Sam wasn't a southerner with all that hospitality, she may have left him in prison, but she also understood his need to find and protect his mate." Kenna squeezed his hand. "You probably would all do the same if in the same boat...not the freaking Pepper out part, but most of the rest."

Gunnar chuckled. "Já. Ari's relationship with Pepper has been the hardest to fix so far...mostly because Connall wants to kill him whenever they are in the same room."

"Probably even when they're not," Kenna added.

"That too."

The car began to wind its way up a very steep hill and Kenna felt a little nauseous.

"You're a little carsick, hmm?" Gunnar laid his hand on her belly and the sick feeling went away.

Kenna let out a sigh of relief. "Thank you." They drove over a drawbridge of sorts and Kenna couldn't keep the awe from her voice as she said, "Wow."

The huge house came into view, and it almost didn't look real.

"It was built into the side of a cliff for safety purposes," Gunnar explained. "It can't be seen from the sky unless you fly right beside it."

"It's amazing."

"Já. I think so too."

Several other "residences" had been built around the main house, all connected to the mansion via underground tunnels. As the driver pulled up to the main house, Kenna couldn't contain a gasp. "It's so festive."

"More so than normal," Gunnar said. "Jesska's been busy."

The giant stone house appeared before them. The four white-washed pillars sat proudly in front, slightly obscuring the porch that ran the entire length of the house. The pillars had been wrapped with live ivy and holly leaves, little white lights artfully woven in between.

Gunnar helped Kenna from the car and they headed into the house. Two large wreaths hung on the front doors and a family of wooden reindeer decorated the front porch. The stone from the porch carried into the foyer; however it was intermixed with river rock. Staircases up each side of the wall met in the middle and created a landing overlooking the open space. Lighted garland wove up the banisters, along with red and gold ribbon and white lights. To the left were tall double doors, and a matching pair to the right.

The door to the music room on the right was open and the baby grand piano held court in the spacious room.

"Will you play later?" Kenna asked.

Gunnar smiled. "Kaspar will insist on it. He always does when I'm home."

"I'll add to the pressure, then."

"Okay, elskan."

The room on the left was the formal parlor, but for now, Gunnar guided Kenna to the back of the house and into the kitchen.

"You made it," Jesska exclaimed, and rushed over to hug Kenna, their bellies making it difficult. Jesska was due in just over a month, so they were both moving a little slower.

"Sit down, elskan," Kaspar ordered, and hugged Kenna gently before guiding his mate back to the sofa.

Kaspar had blond hair and wide shoulders like his brother, but where the similarities ended were the eyes. While Kaspar's were green, Gunnar's were a bright blue.

Gunnar kissed Jesska's cheek with a grin. "The house looks lovely."

"Thank you. I would love to take all the credit, but I pretty much just directed traffic..." Jesska frowned at her mate. "...from a chair."

Kaspar smiled. "Which is where you'll do everything from now until the baby comes."

Kenna sat on the sofa and smiled at her sister-in-law. "Perhaps we can convince the boys to take us shopping and wheel us around in wheelchairs."

"Perhaps we can blow this joint and shop without them hovering," Jesska countered.

"Perhaps we can stop grumbling and let our mates take care of us," Kaspar retorted.

Kenna giggled, accepting the cup of tea Gunnar handed her before taking his seat next to her. "Thanks, love."

"Are your parents coming for the holiday?" Gunnar asked Jesska.

"Yes. They get here next week. Cameron's even coming, which is a surprise. I didn't think he'd be able to get the time."

Cameron's her brother, Gunnar provided.

"When do Ari and Megan arrive?" Kenna asked.

"Tomorrow," Kaspar said as he sat next to Jesska and wrapped an arm around her waist. "The MacMillans are coming as well. Pepper is the holdout from Ari's children."

"Translation: Connall is the holdout," Jesska said.

Kenna smiled. "Those men have never spent Christmas apart from one another, at least, other than the time Brodie was in the air force, so I can't imagine they'll start now. Don't take it personally."

"We aren't," Jesska said with a grin. "Ari, on the other hand..."

"Will get over it," Gunnar said. "Besides, I have a feeling we'll all be in Scotland next year."

"Oh, yes, Kaspar said you're building a house there."

Kenna nodded. "Gunnar wore me down."

"And that was so hard to do," he droned sarcastically.

Kenna laughed. "Yes, building a home less than a mile from my sister, getting to design it from the ground up, and spend gobs of money decorating it. Poor me."

"Will you have stables?" Jesska asked.

Gunnar nodded. "Definitely. It might not be right away, but Max has offered to assist me when I'm ready. I may export a couple of our horses and breed them in Scotland."

"Are you going to take Kenna down to see your horses?" Kaspar asked.

"If she's up to it," Gunnar said.

"I'm up to it." Kenna smiled even though she fought back exhaustion as she leaned against him.

"Not today though," Gunnar said.

She giggled. "No, probably not today."

"Why don't you both get settled?" Jesska said. "We'll plan on dinner here tomorrow night, but otherwise, we're keeping the schedule really flexible."

"That sounds perfect."

"When do Nevin and his family arrive?"

"Day after tomorrow." Kenna bit back a yawn. "Sorry. Flying always wipes me out."

"Let's get to our rooms and you can rest a bit." Gunnar kissed her temple. "I have some e-mails to respond to anyway."

"Don't get up," Kaspar ordered when Jesska shifted.

"I was going to walk them out."

"I know where we're going," Gunnar countered. "You rest."

"You know what, brother, how about you be on my side?" Jesska grumbled.

Gunnar laughed as he rose to his feet. "This *is* me being on my side."

"Well, you suck at it."

Kaspar leaned down and kissed Jesska, stroking her cheek and saying something obviously private...her blush said everything.

"Let's get you into bed." Gunnar helped Kenna off the sofa and then guided her through the back of the house and into a large room with several doors.

"I feel like I'm in a hobbit hole," Kenna said with a giggle.

The walls were rounded, which gave the hallway a burrow-type feel.

"Já, it does," Gunnar agreed with a grin, pulling out a key and opening the door directly in front of them.

"Where are you taking me, big man?"

"To my dungeon, young damsel." He stepped back and guided Kenna through the door.

She clapped her hands. "Ooh, goody."

He grinned, taking her hand and leading her through the lighted hallway.

"Did you blow through the mountain?" she asked.

"Já. There are six tunnels leading to several residences used by the family. One extra is used by the staff to get to their homes in the village."

Kenna let her gaze wander, confident in the knowledge that Gunnar would keep her from tripping over anything. The walls and ceiling were forged out of the stone of the mountain and sconces that had been replaced with electric lights still held an ancient feel.

A few hundred yards down the tunnel, Gunnar released her hand in order to unlock another door and then again stepped back.

Kenna walked through and gasped. "Oh, my word."

She'd just stepped into a world of stunning opulence countered by a homey feel. Gunnar wrapped an arm around her from behind and moved her further into the room. "This is our home, sweetheart."

They were standing in a giant great room with three picture windows that overlooked the snowy ground outside. The vaulted ceiling held the biggest chandelier she'd ever seen, and a two-sided fireplace broke the room into two areas. One for reading, with overstuffed chairs and small game tables. On the other side was a large, flat-screen television with a sectional that could seat about six people comfortably. "I feel like I'm in one of those American log homes, only on steroids."

"Is that a good thing?"

"Aye, love, it's a very good thing."

"Good," he said, and chuckled. "Because I just finished the renovation ten years ago and I love it, but we could change it if you don't."

"I don't want to change a thing...but back up. How is this our home?"

"Because it was mine. Ari and I both have homes here, and now this one is ours." He turned her to face him and kissed her. "Come. I'll give you the tour."

The tour took almost thirty minutes, and Kenna knew she'd want to be here as often as possible. The kitchen, although large, was the place that the chef and his assistants spent most of their time, so it was more of a commercial-grade space, but still very pretty.

There were six bedrooms, seven bathrooms, almost ten-thousand square feet of space, but Gunnar saved the best for last. Leading Kenna back downstairs, he took her back to the great room and over to the windows. He pointed out to the right. "Just past the fences there, it's hard to see with all the snow, but our stables are there. I'll take you out there tomorrow."

"I can't wait." She leaned against him watching the snow. "I wish we could ride."

He stroked her hair. "As soon as you have the baby, we'll go, yeah?"

"I would love that."

"For now, sweetheart, it's time for you to rest."

She nodded. "Okay."

Kenna followed him upstairs and changed into one of his oversized T-shirts before burrowing into the beyond comfortable bed, falling asleep almost immediately.

CHAPTER TEN

"KENNA?" GUNNAR CALLED up the stairs.

I'm not ready.

He grinned. *Elskan, we are already late.*

"But I'm a whale," she said from the top of stairs.

Gunnar frowned and rushed up to meet her. "You're not a whale, sweetheart. You're my beautiful, glorious, sexy, pregnant mate."

"Who's as big as a whale."

"Stop it," he ordered. "You're beautiful, Kenna. You'll not speak that way about my mate."

"Everything has changed in just three weeks!" she continued.

"How so?"

She threw her hands in the air. "We were shagging like rabbits back then. Now it's virtually impossible to lie on a shag rug, let alone enjoy it."

Gunnar tried to stop himself from laughing, but failed.

"It's no' funny, Gunnar!"

"Já, elskan, 'tis a bit." He kissed her gently. "We'll be back to shagging in no time. In the meantime, we don't have to stay for long...it is Jesska's family after all. We'll have plenty of time to spend with them."

She sighed. "I feel like we should stay as long as we can."

"*Your* family arrives tomorrow, are you not looking forward to that?"

"Aye, I am. I'm just not quite ready for Christmas. I'm not even done shopping." She gripped his arm. "Angus is the hardest to buy for."

"Fiona should be able to help you."

"Oh, thank you, love, why didn't I think of that?" she droned, sarcastically.

He chuckled. "What did she say when you asked?"

Kenna shrugged. "She had no clue."

"Right then. Let me buy for the men in both our families and you buy for the women."

She bit her lip, considering his suggestion. "That's actually a really good idea."

"I know, sweetheart."

Kenna patted his cheek. "You're both smart and cute. Winning combination, love."

Gunnar grinned. "You're very lucky to have bonded with me."

"Don't I know it." She started down the stairs. "Okay, we're late. Let's go."

Gunnar stopped her and moved in front of her. Once downstairs, he followed her through the door to the tunnel and locked it behind him. "You know, you still haven't let me know about sleeping arrangements. If you want your family to stay with us, they can, Kenna. Just say the word."

"I'm still deciding. We'll talk to them and find out what they want to do."

Gunnar nodded and unlocked the next door, leading back into the hobbit hole. They continued into the main house and Kenna let out a little squeak to find Payton speaking with Jesska. "You came!"

Payton laughed as she wrapped her arms around her sister. "Surprise!"

"I thought you'd be with the Gunnachs."

"She is," Samantha said as she came into Kenna's sight.

"You're here too?" Kenna hugged her while Gunnar headed off to find the men.

"Everyone's here. I think most of Scotland has descended upon this very small fishing town."

"What about your family?"

"We were just in Georgia for Thanksgiving, and my parents decided they wanted to go somewhere warm for Christmas, so they're off to the Bahamas."

"Sacrilege," Kenna retorted.

"Right?" Samantha shivered. "The thought of sunshine and heat is hard, but on Christmas? No thank you." She giggled. "Dalton opted for the sunshine, the beast, so he's joining our parents."

"Well, I for one am so happy you're here." Kenna grinned. "Where are Connall and Pepper?"

"They're getting their kids down. Cody doesn't like change, so Connall is the only one who can get him past the different sleeping space," Samantha said. "Kade, Brodie, and Kaspar are in Kaspar's office, I think, and my kids are asleep upstairs. We brought a couple of nannies with us to help with the brood."

"Good idea," Kenna said.

"Angus and Fi are coming in tomorrow, right?" Samantha asked.

"Aye. With Gillian. Nevin and his family are coming as well."

"Full house." Samantha chuckled. "We're going to have so much fun."

"Yes, yes we are."

Samantha smiled. "How are you feeling?"

"Huge."

She giggled. "That's normal. If you want me to do a quick check before Gillian gets here, I'll be happy to."

Samantha became a research physician when she was human and, since her conversion, she was making strides in researching the differences between human and Cauld Ane blood, along with the treating of human diseases using Cauld Ane blood. But beyond that, she was a gifted doctor, as was Kade, and together they were pretty awe-inspiring.

"I would like that, Samantha," Gunnar piped in.

"Where did you come from?" Kenna accused.

He chuckled, wrapping an arm around her waist. "She's having difficulty breathing."

"I'm not really. I feel great right now."

"May I?" Sam hovered a hand over Kenna's stomach. Kenna nodded and Sam laid both hands on her belly. "Our babies are typically bigger than most human babies, so they run out of room really quickly. When you feel short of breath, I've found that if you lie on your side, you feel some relief." She continued to run her hands over Kenna's abdomen. "He's right where he needs to be, Kenna, so you feel good to me, but I think you might deliver early."

"I'm good with that," she said.

"I feel ya." Sam giggled. "You might just have a Christmas baby, honey. What an amazing gift that would be."

Kenna laid her hands over her belly and leaned back against Gunnar, who kissed her temple. "That would be pretty incredible."

"You should sit down, elskan," Gunnar ordered.

"Yes, you should," Samantha echoed. "Kaspar relegated Jesska to the sofa not long ago, you should join her."

"Teaming up isn't very nice," Kenna grumbled.

Samantha just smiled while Gunnar led Kenna away.

"Oh, look, company," Jesska quipped as Kenna sat beside her.

Kenna couldn't help but giggle. "I have never been this idle in my life."

"You and me both, sister."

"Can I get either of you something to drink?" Gunnar asked.

"Scotch," Kenna said, at the same time Jesska said, "Wine."

"And now that we're back in the real world," Gunnar continued. "Tea?"

Kenna smiled up at him. "Yes, please, love. Thanks."

"I'm fine, Gunnar," Jesska said, also smiling. "But thank you."

Gunnar walked away and Kenna faced Jesska. "Did you talk to Kas about shopping?"

Jesska nodded. "He's happy to drive us down to Patreksfjörður for a few hours if that's okay with you."

"Since I know nothing about it, I'm sure it'll be perfect."

Jesska giggled. "It's not far, but since there's really nothing here, it's a safer bet. I ordered a few things and had them shipped to Megan earlier this month, so I don't have much to buy."

"I bought a few things and wrapped them here as well, so it's all good."

"I talked to Samantha about doing a secret Santa thing, so she's writing up everyone's name and we'll pull names once everyone arrives tomorrow. None of the adults planned ahead for gifts, other than for the kids."

"That's a great idea...considering I didn't plan for the adults either." Kenna grinned. "And it takes so much stress out of it."

"I know. It was actually Megan's idea. She's so good at all that kind of crap."

"I've really liked getting to know them over the last year," Kenna said. "It's so nice to have them so close."

"I miss them. A lot." Jesska sighed. "I can't wait until my parents arrive. Although, they don't get here until the twentieth, but the thought of spending so much time together is a little nerve wracking."

"How come?"

"Before Kaspar, I was getting ready to be engaged to my high school boyfriend, but he was murdered before we could even technically get engaged."

Kenna gasped. "Oh, Jess, I'm so sorry."

"It's all good now. I'm not sad anymore...not for me, anyway. But I had a major cutting issue and nearly killed myself during a particularly dark moment. My parents committed me, because at seventeen, they could."

"They were obviously concerned about you."

"Yes, but I couldn't it see it back then. I didn't speak to them for a long time."

Kenna squeezed her hand.

"Kaspar's made me see that they were doing what they thought was best." She gave Kenna a sad smile. "Megan and Cameron tried to tell me as well back in the day, but there's nothing quite like your mate to set you straight."

Kenna chuckled. "Ain't that the truth."

"Anyway, it's still weird, but we're all trying to work past it and get back the closeness we once had."

"You'll do it, Jess."

"Thanks."

Gunnar arrived with a cup of tea and some of Kenna's favorite shortbread biscuits. "Are those Walker's?" she asked.

"Já, elskan. Payton brought them."

"I love you, Payton," Kenna called out even though she didn't know where she was.

"Love you too," Payton returned.

"I'm going to find my brother," Gunnar said, leaning down to kiss Kenna gently. "Just call me if you need me."

"I will, love. Thanks for the tea."

He smiled and walked away just as Payton flopped down beside her sister. "I could not get your beast of a nephew to go to sleep," she complained.

Kenna grimaced. "Uh-oh."

"I swear that kid knows his cousins are next door and all he wants to do is play."

"You didn't bring a nanny?" Kenna asked.

"Not one who can lift a small house."

Jesska dropped her head back and laughed. "Ohmigod, Payton."

She shrugged. "He eats like every hour. It's insane. And he's as tall as a five-year-old human. But he's always been a great eater and lousy sleeper. At least Pepper feels my pain somewhat. Cody was the same, but not Samantha. *No.* She has perfect wee children who feed every three to four hours, and Phineas has been sleeping through the night since he was six weeks old! Wee ratbag."

"Have a biscuit," Kenna retorted, and handed her the shortbread.

Payton giggled and took a bite. "Thank you."

"Is he down now?" Jesska asked.

"Yes and if the nanny can't get him to calm if he wakes, Brodie's up, so I have some relief for a couple of hours."

"So...you're waiting a bit to have another, then?" Kenna predicted.

"Aye. When he's eighteen, we'll talk."

Jesska laughed. "Good luck with that."

The rest of the afternoon flew by for Kenna and she relaxed more and more as time went on. She couldn't wait for the rest of the festivities to commence. They had a lot of plans over the next two weeks and felt like she'd burst with the excitement of it all.

CHAPTER ELEVEN

THE NEXT MORNING, Kenna was awake before Gunnar. This was such a strange phenomenon that she decided to surprise him with breakfast. Arriving downstairs, she put on a pot of coffee and pulled out everything she'd need for omelets. If she'd thought the kitchen in Reykjavík was a dream, then this one was a waking fantasy. For a man who didn't cook, he certainly knew how to outfit a kitchen.

Elskan, where are you?

Kenna smiled as she cracked eggs into a bowl. *Serving my man.*

You should be resting.

Come and taste my omelets and then *tell me that.*

Gunnar walked into the kitchen a few minutes later, glorious in his pajama bottoms that sat low on his hips and a white singlet. Kenna stopped her whisking for a second to admire him. "Good morning, gorgeous."

He smiled, walking around the island to kiss her. "Good morning." He hunkered down in front of her and kissed her belly. "How's our son?"

"He's doing cartwheels right now because he knows you're talking to hm."

"Sit down, elskan."

"I'm fine, love. I feel great." She stroked his cheek. "Why don't you pour the coffee? I've brewed a pot."

"Then you'll sit down?"

She giggled. "I'll sit down when I'm done and leave the dishes to you."

He rose to his feet and kissed her again. "I can live with that."

"Good."

Kenna hummed as she prepared omelets and bacon, along with fresh fruit she'd found in the fridge. Whoever had done the shopping had done a thorough job of stocking up on whatever they would need.

As soon as she'd slid Gunnar's omelet onto his plate, he grabbed both plates. "You sit down. I'll do the rest," he ordered.

Kenna picked up the coffee mugs and smiled. "Thank you."

He followed her to the large kitchen table and set a plate in front of her before gathering utensils and joining her. Kenna sipped her coffee as Gunnar took a bite and swallowed. "*Ljúffengur*, elskan."

"I'm glad you like it." Seconds later, Kenna felt pain in her abdomen and took a deep breath.

"Kenna?" Gunnar reached for her, but she shook her head.

"I'm okay, love. He's just moving around."

Gunnar stood and picked her up out of her seat. "What are you doing?" she squeaked, barely saving her coffee mug from shattering on the ground.

"You are going to rest and there will be no more making breakfast until after you have the baby."

"Gunnar," she admonished as he continued up the stairs with her. "This is all normal. I'm healthy, the baby's healthy. You can't lock me away because I feel like a beached whale right now."

"I'm going to have Samantha come and check on you."

"Gillian will be here in less than two hours, don't bug Sam."

He set her on the bed and frowned. "On your side, sweetheart. Like Sam said."

She stretched out, reaching for his hand. "I'm okay, love."

He linked his fingers with hers at the same time he pulled his phone out and put it to his ear. "Kaz, já, *Kenna líður ekki vel. Gætirðu beðið Sam að koma, vinsamlegast? Fylgdu henni beint upp í svefnherbergið okkar? Já, þakka þér.*" (Kenna's not feeling well. Could you ask Sam to come please? Escort her straight to our bedroom? Yes. Thank you.)

Kenna closed her eyes and took several deep breaths. *I really am okay, Gunnar.*

"Humor me," he said, and grabbed clothes to change into.

More pain rolled through her but she tried not to react, however, that didn't go so well for her.

"Ansans," Gunnar hissed.

"I'm okay, I'm okay."

"You're not okay," he accused, sitting beside her and laying his hand on her belly. "I can feel your pain."

"That helps," Kenna said, and licked her lips. "Keep doing that."

A knock at the door brought Kade and Samantha.

"You're not well, Kenna?" Samantha asked as she stepped to the bed.

"I'm fine. Just a little pain."

"Okay, honey, let's have you roll on your back," Samantha directed. "Gunnar, can you move to the other side, please. Keep contact with her...it'll help."

Gunnar climbed over Kenna and helped her onto her back. The pain shot through her legs and back and she couldn't stop a whimper.

"I've got you," Gunnar whispered, kissing her fingers.

Samantha felt Kenna's belly, then pulled out her stethoscope and listened before turning to Kade. "The baby's heartbeat is slowing."

"What does that mean?" Kenna demanded.

"It means if we can't get him regulated, we're going to need to get him out."

"I'll get supplies," Kade said. "Be right back."

"Thanks, baby," Samantha said, and squeezed Kenna's arm. "We're going to get you undressed, okay? I think you're going to have your baby today."

"I can't," Kenna argued. "Everyone's coming."

"Kaspar will take care of your family, sweetheart," Gunnar assured her as he helped her undress. "You focus on you and the baby."

Kenna felt a rush of wet and cried out.

"It's okay, honey," Samantha crooned. "Your water broke. You're definitely having this baby today. Gunnar, Kade is bringing ice sheets, so why don't you lift her into the chair for a bit while I get this bedding off."

Gunnar nodded and gently lifted Kenna off the bed, wrapping a blanket around her and carrying her to the chair by the bed. He settled her on his lap and she buried her face in his neck, trying to take deep breaths as the pain overtook her body.

"You're having our baby, elskan," he whispered, stroking her hair.

He's early.

"I know, baby, but it's going to be fine."

She shook her head. *He's too early.*

No, he's right on time.

Kenna forced back tears as she focused on her breathing. "Everything hurts."

"We'll get you comfortable in just a minute," Samantha promised. "Kade, grab that side, will you please?"

"Aye," he answered.

Kenna hadn't even heard the king return. She suddenly felt it difficult to breathe and gripped Gunnar's arm as another wave of pain rocked her. "I can't," she rasped.

"Gunnar, let's get her on the ice," Samantha said. "She'll feel better."

Gunnar lifted her and gently laid her on the bed. Kenna felt the pain leave as the cold wrapped around her. "Thank you."

"Let's hear that baby." Samantha laid the stethoscope diaphragm over Kenna's belly and smiled. "Much better, Kenna. He's way more comfortable. If you want to roll on your side, you might feel better."

Kenna nodded and did as she suggested, sliding her hand into Gunnar's. He faced her, laying his head on the pillow opposite hers. Sam pulled the top sheet over her for modesty and then she and Kade moved around the room, quietly prepping for the imminent arrival of the baby.

"I think his name has much more significance now," Kenna whispered.

Gunnar chuckled. "Já. Styrr is most definitely a little warrior."

Kenna smiled, closing her eyes. "I'm so tired."

"Sleep, hon," Samantha said, and laid her hand on Kenna's arm. "He'll wake you when he's ready to come."

* * *

Gunnar waited for Kenna to fall asleep before sitting up. "Is she okay? Is the baby?"

"Yes, Gunnar." Samantha smiled. "She's much better now that she's cooler." She checked her watch. "Gillian will be here in less than half an hour, so you've got one kickass OB and two other not so bad doctors on your side."

"Speak for yourself," Kade retorted.

Samantha giggled. "Okay, one kickass OB, a kickass general practitioner, and me."

Kade frowned, but Samantha just patted his chest and smiled up at him. "You're ridiculous," she whispered.

He nodded. "So you keep telling me."

Gunnar watched his mate as she slept, his worry somewhat eased as Kade and Samantha prepped the room a little more. Gillian breezed in twenty minutes later, concern etched in the tightness of her features as she walked to the bed.

"Oh, she's asleep. Good," she said with a sigh. "That's a good sign. Did one of you check her?"

Samantha shook her head. "Her water broke and shortly after she fell asleep, so we decided to wait."

"I should check her now."

"Can we let her sleep?" Gunnar asked.

Before Gillian could answer, Kenna came awake with a scream, grabbing for Gunnar as she cried out in pain.

"Kenna, love, it's Gillie. Listen to my voice." Gillian took her sister's hand. "I need you to roll over. I'm going to check you, love."

Kenna grasped Gunnar's arm. "No, I can't."

"You can, elskan," Gunnar crooned. "I'm here. I've got you."

Gillian pulled on gloves as Gunnar helped Kenna onto her back. He tried not to panic when he felt her pain seconds before she cried out again.

"Something's wrong," Kenna rasped.

Gillian laid one hand on her belly and checked her with the other. "The baby's turned himself around, Kenna. We're going to have to turn him the right way so he can come." She glanced up at Samantha. "She's fully dilated and effaced, we need to do this quickly."

"We're ready," Samantha said.

The women turned the baby as gently as they could, but Gunnar thought he might lose his mind at the depths of Kenna's pain. It knocked the wind out of him as he tried to take it from her.

"Ansans," he hissed out as they pressed on Kenna's stomach.

Kenna screamed, but then just as quickly as they'd started, they stopped, and Gillian nodded, smiling at her sister. "He's good, love. He's ready to come, so when a contraction hits, push."

"Drugs. I want drugs."

"It's too late for drugs, sis. I'm sorry."

"I hate you!" Kenna screamed as a contraction hit and she grabbed her knees for leverage to push.

"Gunnar, get behind her so you can support her," Gillian ordered.

Gunnar did as he was told, settling Kenna's back to his chest and kissing her temple. "Use me to anchor you, elskan."

Kenna dropped her head back onto his shoulder. "I can't do this..." She cried out and gripped Gunnar's hands as she pushed again.

"That's it, love," Gillian encouraged. "We can see the head. One more big push, Kenna. You can do it."

It took ten minutes and three more strong pushes for Styrr Gunnarsson to make his entrance into the world. He was one week early and still weighed nine pounds, six ounces, and was twenty-one inches long.

"Well done, Kenna," Gillian crooned as she held the baby for Gunnar to cut the cord. She set Styrr on Kenna's chest and helped clean Kenna up.

"Och, he's perfect," Kenna whispered. "Our little prince."

"Já, baby, he is." Gunnar kissed his wife's temple as he stroked the baby's back.

"Kade and I will check him out, Kenna, okay? Then you can have him back."

Kenna handed the baby off to Samantha and Gillian tapped her leg. "You're starting to heal, love. You'll feel a little euphoric in a minute, then you'll crash a bit. While you're feeling up to it, we're going to change the sheets, okay?"

Kenna nodded and relaxed against Gunnar. Gunnar felt her body change and lifted her off the bed. "She's good," he said.

Gillian made quick work of changing the bedding and Gunnar had Kenna back under the covers within minutes, just as he felt her mood shift. Samantha settled a swaddled Styrr in Kenna's arms and helped to get him latched onto her breast. "Well, look at him go," Samantha crooned. "He's obviously a prince *and* a genius."

"Thanks, Sam," Kenna said as she smiled down at her son.

"We'll get out of your hair now. We'll fill your family in on everything and you guys can have some private time."

"Thank you," Gunnar said. "Both of you."

Kade smiled with a nod and followed Samantha out of the room.

"Right, love." Gillian smiled. "I'll sort out the family so you can bond a little, eh?"

"I wrote down room options," Kenna said.

"It's all good, Kenna, we'll find our way." Gillian rose to her feet and leaned over to kiss her sister and nephew. "Bless you and your new family. I'll be back in a little while to check on you."

"Thanks, sis."

Gillian left the room and Gunnar focused on the beauty and miracle that was his family. "I love you, sweetheart."

"I love you too."

* * *

Three days later, the family were all together at Kaspar's enormous dining room table. Kenna had just fed a sleepy Styrr and settled him in the bassinet between her and

Gunnar. Niall and Charlotte had surprised everyone by arriving along with Gillian, Angus, and Fiona. Nevin and his family had arrived the day before.

Max and Grace now had two children and were in the States with her family, and although Charlotte and Niall had been invited as well, Charlotte wanted to be with her sisters this holiday, especially to show off their new wee son, Taran.

"Since it is the twelfth of December, tonight is the night Stekkjarstaur is scheduled to arrive. He will be the first Yule lad to come," Ari said, and turned to his daughter. "So, elskan, you must put a shoe in the window."

Ari had long, blond hair that he'd pulled away from his face, looking much like a Viking warrior and less like the brooding artist he was deep down.

"Papa, I'm almost nineteen," Sophia argued.

"Já, but you don't want a potato, so you'll put a shoe in the window."

"Humor him, sweetpea," Megan instructed. "It's his first Christmas with you and your sisters in one place. He's making up for lost time."

Sophia rolled her eyes. "But I need all my shoes, Mom. And what if *he*...I mean, this dude Stek-whatever *does* put a potato in my shoe? I'm gonna be kind of annoyed." She shuddered. "Gross."

Chuckles pittered around the table.

"You can avoid potatoes by doing what your Papa tells you," Ari said.

"I'm not six."

Ari raised an eyebrow. "You're still my baby."

Sophia stared at her father and then gave him a beaming smile. "Papa?"

"Já, elskan."

"If you put a potato in my shoe—"

"If *Stekkjarstaur* puts—"

"Yeah, whatever. If Stekkjarstaur puts a potato in my shoe, I'm going to put glue in yours. Capisce?"

Kenna covered her mouth to keep from laughing out loud. Good lord, the girl was funny.

Ari did laugh, leaning down to kiss his daughter's head. "I'm still your father, little one, remember that."

"Um, Dad?" Pepper pointed to him with her knife. "The three of us together can nail you to the wall...literally, so how about you remember that. Right, Charlotte?"

Charlotte raised her hands in surrender. "Leave me out of this one, darling sisters. I am Switzerland."

"Chicken," Pepper accused.

"How many of these little devils do we have to contend with?" Megan asked.

"Tomorrow, Giljagaur comes," Ari said. "Then there's Stúfur, Þvörusleikir, Pottaskefill, Askasleikir, Hurðaskellir, Skyrgámur, Bjúgnakrækir, Gluggagægir, Gáttaþefur, Kertasníkir, and finally, Ketkrókur."

"Swap those," Kaspar corrected. "Ketkrókur, then, Kertasníkir."

Ari smiled. "Right."

"So basically one each night until Christmas?" Sophia asked. "Which means, several chances for potatoes to be put in our shoes?"

"Já, elskan."

"It's like Elf on a Shelf," Megan said.

"Didn't Uncle Cameron murder that little elf?" Sophia asked.

"That was my fault," Megan admitted. "The book came out and I loved the idea of it, so I attempted to try it with you, which meant Cameron had to play along."

"But I was like, seven."

"I know, honey. Cameron also used that argument." She giggled. "In the end it was a bust, but maybe we can try with the wee ones."

"We'll do the boot and the elf," Jesska suggested.

"This is child abuse," Sophia grumbled. "Or at the very least, manipulation."

Megan laughed. "Hey, whatever works, my little imp."

"What? I was a perfect angel."

Jesska choked on her water. "We're going with that?" she asked, once she caught her breath.

Sophia rolled her eyes.

"Soph, how about you help Moira put one of her shoes in the window?" Charlotte suggested.

Sophia grinned at Moira. "Do you want auntie Sophia to help you?"

"'K," Moira said. "Now?"

"After dinner, baby," Niall said.

"But Taran's the baby."

He grinned. "Aye, lass, but you'll always be *my* baby."

Her cheeks pinkened and she leaned against him. "'K, Da."

All the women let out a collective sigh. There was nothing sweeter than a man who adored his daughter, and the hero worship in her face was evident.

"I love the little Scottish accent she's got going on," Megan said.

Charlotte nodded. "I do too."

The rest of the evening was spent gathering the children's shoes and finding enough windowsill space to fit them all on.

CHAPTER TWELVE

CHRISTMAS EVE MORNING, Kenna awoke to pressure in her breasts...and not in a good way, especially since Gunnar wasn't in bed with her. *Gunnar?*

"Our son will not settle, elskan."

Kenna sat up and smiled. Gunnar held a screaming Styrr in his arms and he was rocking him gently. Gunnar had offered to get him so she could sleep, but it seemed Styrr was having none of it. She reached for him. "I'm engorged, love, so hand him to me. He's obviously hungry."

Gunnar laid him in Kenna's arms, kissing her gently and then a little more thoroughly once she got Styrr comfortable.

She reached up and stroked his cheek. "How long have you been awake?"

"I made him a bottle at three and then he woke again thirty minutes ago, but he wouldn't take a bottle." He sat on the edge of the mattress and patted Styrr's back.

Kenna stroked Styrr's head. "I can't figure out who's more obsessed with my breasts, my wee lad. You or your da."

Gunnar chuckled. "Me. Definitely."

Kenna giggled. "My wee prince, you need to be good today. Aðfangadagur starts at six and you get to open your presents."

"I'm sure we'll help him open them. I'm convinced our son is a genius, but I believe opening packages might be out of the realm of his abilities just yet."

"You may have a point." Kenna laughed again. "I still think it's weird to open all your presents on Christmas Eve."

"You do?"

"Yes. We have always done it on Christmas morning." Last year they'd done the same.

"Next year we can do both," Gunnar said.

"Perfect." Kenna focused back on Styrr.

"Tomorrow is Jóladagur," Gunnar said. "We'll have lamb in the evening, but the afternoon will be making Laufabrauð."

"Have you come up with a pattern?"

Kenna learned last year that Laufabrauð, leaf bread, was made of thin sheets of dough cut into delicate patterns and fried. Each family often had their own design, and she and Gunnar had been trying to come up with something unique, but ended up just frying round pieces of dough. This year, she hoped they could be a little more creative.

Gunnar rose from the bed with a nod and pulled open his nightstand drawer, pulling out a piece of paper and handing it to her. "What do you think?"

He'd drawn a tree with three branches and room for more as their family grew. "Och, honey, it's beautiful. Will we be able to recreate it?"

He grinned. "Easy."

"I'll leave that part to you. If I tried to do it, it would end up looking like a headless person."

Gunnar laughed. "You can't be that bad."

"Challenge accepted," she retorted, and moved Styrr to her other side.

"I'm going to take a quick shower and then we'll have breakfast, sound good?"

Kenna nodded. "Perfect, love."

Gunnar headed to the shower and Kenna finished up with Styrr.

* * *

Kenna settled Styrr in his bassinet then joined Jesska in the kitchen. A handsome, tall, dark-haired man was loading the dishwasher. "Kenna, this is my brother, Cameron. Cam, this is Kenna. Gunnar's wife."

Kenna shook his hand. "It's lovely to meet you."

"You too," Cameron said.

"Cam, can you come help me please?" a deep voice called.

Cameron grinned. "Dad needs help doing something secret...which means, he might burn the house down. I better go. Excuse me."

"Make sure he doesn't flood anything either," Jess ordered to his retreating back.

"Got it," Cameron replied.

Kenna smiled, leaning against the counter. "How do you feel, Jess?"

Jesska rubbed her belly. "Sore."

"You should really rest."

"Ohmigod, Kenna, don't you start too," she accused. "Between Kaz and my mom, I might slap someone."

Kenna gave her a gentle hug. "I'm sorry, Jess. I know it's hard, but if you're having pains, you should at least—"

"Jesska Marie," her mother snapped as she walked into the room. "Get off your feet."

"See," she whispered, rolling her eyes.

"I was just taking her over to the sofa," Kenna said.

"Thank you, Kenna," Jesska's mother said. "You're a good friend."

Kenna smiled and looped her arm with Jesska's. "Does Kaspar know you're up?"

"What the hell are you doing on your feet?" Kaspar growled, walking toward them, having come from his office.

Kenna grimaced. "That would be a 'no.'"

"Ten more seconds and I would have been in the clear," Jesska grumbled.

"I knew you were up to something when you tried to block me," Kaspar accused (albeit in a quieter voice due to human ears) and wrapped an arm around her waist. "Do you want to go back to bed?"

"Oh, calm down, your Highness, I'm going," Jesska breathed out.

Kenna gave Jesska a bolstering smile as Kaspar made sure she sat down. He took a seat next to her and linked his fingers with hers.

"Why are you staring at my brother?" Gunnar whispered, kissing the back of her neck.

Kenna jumped, spinning to face him. "You need to stop doing that."

He chuckled, kissing her nose. "Sorry. Now, why are you staring at my brother?"

"Just watching him with Jess." She wove her arms around his neck. "She's so frustrated and I get it, but now I realize I may have put you through a little more hell than I should have. I'm sorry I didn't listen to you more."

He pulled her close and kissed her forehead. "You're forgiven. But may I remind you of this conversation when you're pregnant with our next baby?"

Before she could respond, Styrr let out a bellow that started a domino effect with the other babies in the room.

"Shite," Kenna whispered, and dropped her arms, rushing to pick up the baby. "Hey, little prince. What's going on? I only fed you twenty minutes ago." She held him close and rocked him. "Let's check your nappy, then we'll see if you need to eat more."

Kenna changed his diaper and then found a quiet place to feed him. The other children were settled and then the nannies took over.

Christmas gifts were exchanged and Kenna got caught up in the excitement of the children. Luckily, the main house was big enough for the kids to play without doing too much damage. By midnight, Kenna was having a hard time keeping her eyes open, so Gunnar insisted they head home."

"We'll see you in the morning," Payton said, hugging her. "We'll do our best to keep Killian from waking you before dawn."

"We might be up anyway if Styrr doesn't sleep through the night."

"Okay, well, if you're up, don't let him wake *us*," Payton pleaded.

Kenna giggled. "No problem, sis."

She hugged her family, Gunnar lifted Styrr gently, and they headed home.

CHAPTER THIRTEEN

KENNA AWOKE WITH a start, discombobulated as she tried to sort out the vibration thrumming through her body.

"I'm calling Kaz," Gunnar said.

"It's got to be Jess, if you feel it too," Kenna said, and climbed out of bed.

The Cauld Ane could feel their siblings' emotional highs and lows, albeit with lesser intensity, but now that Kenna was bound to Gunnar, she'd know something was going on. Since Gunnar felt it was Kaspar, Kenna deduced it was probably Jesska instead.

Gunnar set the phone against his ear as he pulled on a pair of jeans. "Já. Já. Okay." He hung up and smiled. "The baby's coming."

Kenna bounced on her feet and clapped quietly. "How exciting! I'll feed Styrr and have Payton watch him while we go help Jess."

"That sounds good."

Once the baby was sorted, Kenna followed Gunnar through the tunnels to the main house and upstairs to where organized chaos was commencing in the master bedroom. Gunnar stayed in the hallway with Ari and Jesska's father and brother, but Kenna slipped inside.

Kaspar was behind Jesska, her back against his chest, anchoring her to him, and she was taking slow, deep breaths. Kade and Samantha were prepping the room, while Gillian pulled on gloves and checked her. Jesska's mother held her hand, unable to really do anything.

"What can I do?" Kenna asked.

"If you can help Megan grab the sheets, I'd appreciate it," Gillian said, careful to be somewhat vague since Jesska's human mother would not understand the need for ice sheets.

"Aye, sis. Be right back." Kenna found Megan, and together they gathered the supplies they'd need.

Thirty minutes later, Jesska cried out as she delivered the new prince. Skúli Kasparson arrived with a quiet cry and a perfectly round head.

"Och, lass, look at how pink he is," Gillian said as she lay the baby on Jesska's chest. "He's perfect."

Jesska let out a tired sigh as she leaned back against Kaspar and stared down at the baby. "Hi there, baby," she whispered. "I'm your mama and that's your daddy. You are so loved, sweet boy."

Samantha took the baby away briefly to weigh and measure him, and then he was back in Jesska's arms just as soon as Gillian had cleared away the dirty sheets and replaced them with clean ones.

Kenna and Megan took a minute to kiss Skúli and Jesska, then they left the new family for some bonding time. Kenna walked out of the room and into Gunnar's arms. "He's perfect. Just over ten pounds, almost twenty-three inches long, and one of the most beautiful children I've ever seen. Jesska was such a warrior."

Gunnar stroked her hair and kissed her temple. "So were you."

Kenna smiled up at him. "Is everyone still asleep?"

"Yes. Do you want to go back to bed?"

She sighed. "Yes, please. I'm sure Megan will fill everyone else in on this end and we'll tell our lot."

He smiled and led her back home.

* * *

The next morning, as early morning light shone through the transom windows of their bedroom, Kenna rolled over and kissed her mate. "Happy Christmas, sweetheart."

"Happy Christmas." He grinned, smiling against her lips. "I love Jóladagur. Especially now."

"Oh?"

He wrapped his arms around her, rolling her onto her back. "There's always been something so special about the morning of Christmas, but having you and Styrr, and now a new little nephew, it just makes everything so much better."

Kenna stroked his face. "I feel the same."

"I have something for you." He kept hold of her while he reached into the drawer of the side table, pulling out a beautifully wrapped box.

Kenna bounced a little as she tore the paper off and opened the box. Inside was an emerald cut topaz ring with matching bracelet. "Gunnar," she whispered.

"Do you like them?"

She shook her head. "I love them."

"You had me scared for a minute." He buried his face her neck, blowing a raspberry and making her giggle.

"Sorry, love," she said. "I have yours as well." Reaching into her side table, she pulled out the watch she'd bought for him. He opened the gift and rolled on his back to hold it up to the light. "You never wear one."

He grinned, slipping it on his wrist. "It's because I've never found one I liked, and since my phone is much like a pocket watch, I've never seen the need." Rolling to face her, he kissed her gently. "It's perfect. I love it." He moved his lips to skim along her jaw and she craned her head to give him better access...just as the baby monitor lit up with Styrr's bellow.

"Your son has the worst timing," Kenna complained as she smiled and climbed out of bed.

Gunnar flopped onto his back and ran his hands through his hair. "No, elskan, *your* son has the worst timing."

Kenna grabbed her robe and slipped into their son's room. "Good morning, little prince," she crooned, lifting him from his crib and cradling him close. "I'm guessing you're hungry, eh?" He sniffed, his bottom lip quivering. "We'll get that nappy off you first, love."

"I'll do that, sweetheart," Gunnar offered, reaching for Styrr.

"I'll just wash my face while you do," she said.

Kenna returned and sat in the rocker to feed the baby. She smiled up at Gunnar, who leaned against the wall and crossed his arms, watching them. "What?"

"I'm just taken by how beautiful you are."

She blushed. "Thank you, love."

"I can't wait to make more babies with you."

Kenna giggled. "Me too, even though I haven't forgotten the last two months."

Gunnar grinned. "We won't travel next time. People will just have to come to us."

"That works for me."

Over the next few days, Kenna reveled in her time with her family. New Year's Eve was the last day the family would be together as a whole, as many were heading back the next day. The non Icelanders were introduced to *Áramótaskaup*, a comedy, year-in-review type show, where actors make fun of political flops and the year's best news.

At midnight, the babies were settled with the nannies, while the adults and little ones were treated to a fireworks show that rivaled anything Kenna had seen in the past. Kaspar had hired a professional company to put the whole thing on, set to music and timed to perfection.

Jesska had arranged big chaise loungers that couples could sit together in, along with comfortable chairs and blankets if people preferred. Gunnar sat in a chair, pulling Kenna between his legs and wrapping his arms around her. She leaned into him, craning her neck to kiss him, and then settling in to watch the show.

Brodie had a hard time keeping hold of Killian, because the now one-year-old toddler kept trying to get to wherever the fireworks were. Payton couldn't control her laughter as he'd elude his father (albeit briefly) and climb something to get as high as he could.

"I think he's going to be a pilot," Brodie said, pulling him down off the trellis at the side of the house.

"He'll have to be," Payton agreed. "Because, if he's not, he'll do something crazy like jump out of planes in an attempt to fly."

Kenna shuddered, snuggling closer to Gunnar. "If Styrr does anything crazier than being a geeky computer nerd, I'll have a heart attack."

Gunnar chuckled. "We'll see."

"We better no' see. I want him safe...always."

"Okay, baby. He'll be safe...always."

"Good answer."

The next installment of the show began and this time, Killian settled down enough to watch. He climbed onto his parents' chaise and cuddled close, falling asleep just before everything ended.

Once everyone said goodnight, Gunnar took Kenna to bed and Styrr slept through the night...however, they didn't. They were working on making a bigger family and Kenna couldn't think of a better reason to be exhausted the next day.

CHAPTER FOURTEEN

THE OFFICIAL LAST day of Christmas fell on the sixth of January, and Gunnar and Kenna returned to Reykjavik the day before in order to celebrate at home. They were expecting Ari, Megan, and Sophia for dinner that evening, and Kenna was taking the time to cook something magnificent.

Another huge fireworks display had been advertised over the water and their apartment had a perfect view, so she was excited to see what they came up with this year. Last year's had been great, but the city had promised something even better this year.

"What are you making?" Gunnar asked, walking into the kitchen with Styrr. "It smells incredible."

"We'll start with a roasted squash soup," she said as she put the squash into the oven. "Then I'm doing grilled pork chops, asparagus, and garlic mashed potatoes. For dessert, I'm making a self-saucing chocolate pudding with cream."

"Seriously?"

"Aye." She smiled up at him. "Why?"

"Because I'm going to get fat."

Kenna giggled. "Well, if you do, I'm doing my job."

"You want me fat?"

She stood on her tiptoes. "If it makes you happy, then yes." Kissing him gently, she smiled, then kissed Styrr's head before returning to her duties.

"*Ég elska þig.*" (I love you.)

"I love you, too."

"I'll put Styrr down and come and help."

"Thanks, love."

Kenna put Gunnar on table setting duty, which probably wasn't the greatest idea. He was a prince, after all, and had never set a table, so she ended up fixing a few things.

Styrr wanted to be fed just as Ari and Megan arrived, so Gunnar took care of getting everyone drinks while Kenna took care of the baby. She changed him and swaddled him tight before carrying him back out to the living room to an eager Megan who was reaching for him. "Gimme."

Kenna giggled and handed the baby off to her.

Megan stroked his cheek. "Hey, little man. Oh, how your auntie misses this time. You are so handsome."

"We can always have another one," Ari said.

Megan smiled. "Let's get Sophia out of the house for good and then we'll talk."

"Ew, Mom, gross. Having a baby at your age?"

"Elskan," Ari admonished.

"What, Papa. My sisters are almost thirty...I'm eighteen. It's weird."

Kenna smiled. "It's weird in your world, love. But not in ours. Once you're bound, you'll understand."

She rolled her eyes. "I am not getting 'bound.'"

"Oh?"

"Sorry, auntie Kenna, but I'm not. Why do the men always have all the power? I want to be able to pick the man I marry."

"It's not like we didn't choose our mates," Kenna said.

"Well, what do you call it, then?" she challenged. "If we are destined to be with one person, then it's not much of a choice."

Ari frowned. "This is why you should have never left."

Megan shook her head. "This is why you shouldn't have lied."

Ari and Megan were destined to mate, but when he met Megan, she was seventeen and human. Their Kalt Einn customs and lore were far more ingrained than even the Cauld Anes', and Ari believed he'd hurt her if he bound her. Megan, fearing she was going insane and in danger, escaped with Sophia, and changed their names in an effort to keep her safe, but Kaspar found them, in turn reuniting Ari and Megan. They were now the family they should have been all along.

"Sorry. I didn't mean to cause a fight," Sophia said. "I just know how I feel."

"And you're entitled to feel however you feel, love," Kenna encouraged. "Just try not to let your emotions shadow your common sense, because one day, you'll find the man you're destined to be with, and you'll choose him. I promise."

"We'll see," Sophia said.

Kenna and Megan shared a secret smile, and then Kenna headed into the kitchen to finish dinner. Megan handed the baby off to Gunnar and joined her a few minutes later.

"Oh, that girl," Megan breathed out as she washed her hands. "She's going to kill me."

Kenna grinned and salted the potatoes. "She'll figure it out."

"I hope so. I have managed to raise a very well-adjusted, independent, confident, and highly opinionated human being. Ari wants to kill her then me most days. She doesn't know what it's like to have a father, and to suddenly have one is an adjustment."

"Is it not going well?"

Megan dried her hands. "No, it's not that, necessarily. Ari missed so much after Charlotte and Pepper were taken from us. More him than me, because he erased my memories, but when I disappeared with Sophia, he missed both of us, so now he has us back, and he's intense. More so than when we were together before. I'm fine with it because we're in sync, but Sophia's not used to it, so she's balking at the over-protectiveness a little. Gotta give my girl credit though, she pushes because she's strong, but she's never disrespectful, and she tries to give Ari one-on-one time whenever she can. This whole not wanting a mate thing is new, so it's going to be interesting to see what happens in the coming years."

Kenna giggled. "I'm kind of glad I have a front row seat to the show."

"You and me both, sister." Megan grinned. "What can I do?"

"Well, we can start carrying food out. I'll have Gunnar get the wine and then we're ready."

Megan nodded and picked up the platter with the chops, carrying it to the table. Once dinner was done, and much to Ari's princely chagrin, Gunnar made him help with the cleanup while Kenna, Styrr, Megan, and Sophia sat out on the balcony waiting for the sun to set.

The men joined them, handing everyone drinks, and then once Styrr was fed and changed, Gunnar set him in the bassinet inside the closed glass doors so they could see him, but where he wouldn't be shocked by the sound of the booms.

The fireworks, although a half hour long, seemed so much shorter. The light display depicted elves and the beautiful people that Icelanders believe live in the rocks and mountains of Iceland. The show told the story of a traditional Icelandic Christmas, and the images of the giantess Grýla and her third husband, Leppalúði ended the show. The sound of clapping echoed from the people standing on their balconies.

After hugs and goodbyes, Ari, Megan, and Sophia left and Kenna carried Styrr to bed, Gunnar following.

As she climbed under the covers and cuddled close to her mate, she was overcome with the blessings she'd been given. She'd waited a long time for Gunnar, but he was more than worth the wait, and she was forever grateful.

"I've waited a long time for you too, elskan."

Kenna giggled. "Much longer than me."

He patted her bottom and kissed her temple. "Are you calling me aged?"

"I would never say that...out loud."

Gunnar rolled her onto her back and hovered above her. "I think I need to show you what this old man can do." She gasped as he cupped her breast. "Yes, please." Gunnar made love to her and she was swept away by a perfect Christmas wish come true.

I was born and raised in New Zealand. With an American father, Scottish grandmother, and Kiwi mother, it's no doubt I have a unique personality.

After pursuing my American roots and disappearing into my time travel series, The Civil War Brides, I thought I'd explore the Scottish side of my family. I have loved delving into the Cauld Ane's and all their abilities... I hope you do too.

I've been happily married and gooey in love with my husband for more than twenty years. We live in the Pacific Northwest with our two sons.

I hope you've enjoyed **Bound by Light**
For other titles in the Cauld Ane Series,
or to learn about The Civil War Brides Series, please visit:
www.traceyjanejackson.com

Find me on Facebook, too!
http://www.facebook.com/traceyjanejackson

If you'd like to read the book Thane and Charlotte's movie was based on, The Bride Price, it's free for download pretty much everywhere, so check your favorite online seller.

Made in the USA
Middletown, DE
18 October 2015